'A beautifully-written and incredibly moving triptych of tales that are so good you'll have to ration yourself.'

... der Teacher ...SchoolBookClub

...ngaging and entertaining.'
Independent on Sunday

'Perfect for captivating the imagination.'
Mumsnet

'Absorbing … brimming with atmospheric detail.'
Carousel

'My go-to author for historical fiction.'
The Bookbag

'Rich in thrilling details.'
Lovereading4kids

'Compelling.'
Metro

'Absorbing, sensitive and genuinely magical in feel.'
Independent

'A fast, exciting read.'
The School Librarian

'If your middle grade kids (ages 8-12) haven't discovered Emma Carroll yet, then they're missing out.'
Irish Times

FABER & FABER

has published children's books since 1929. Some of our very first publications included *Old Possum's Book of Practical Cats* by T. S. Eliot, starring the now world-famous Macavity, and *The Iron Man* by Ted Hughes. Our catalogue at the time said that 'it is by reading such books that children learn the difference between the shoddy and the genuine'. We still believe in the power of reading to transform children's lives.

About the Author

Emma Carroll was a secondary school English teacher before leaving to write full time. She has also worked as a news reporter, an avocado picker and the person who punches holes into filofax paper. She graduated with distinction from Bath Spa University's MA in Writing For Young People. *When We Were Warriors* is Emma's ninth book. She lives in the Somerset hills with her husband and two terriers.

WHEN WE WERE WARRIORS

Emma Carroll

90 YEARS OF EXCELLENCE

FABER & FABER

First published in 2019
by Faber & Faber Limited
Bloomsbury House,
74–77 Great Russell Street,
London WC1B 3DA

Typeset in Garamond Premier by MRules
Printed by CPI Group (UK) Ltd, Croydon CR0 4YY

A CIP record for this book
is available from the British Library

ISBN 978–0–571–35040–7

2 4 6 8 10 9 7 5 3 1

CONTENTS

THE NIGHT
VISITORS

1

At the exact moment the bomb hit, Stan and his sisters were on their way to get chips. They were taking the short cut through the alley that ran behind Pavilion Street. It was unusually late to be out – almost bedtime – so they were hurrying in the hope of catching the chip shop still open. The evening was warm, the sky a lovely soft orange. On nights like these – and there'd been plenty this summer – it was hard to believe there was a war on. June, the eldest, walked in front, swinging Mum's purse so the coins inside clinked. She'd already decided on haddock with her chips. Stan and his younger sister Maggie were debating whether battered sausages or fishcakes were best, and what else they might get with Mum's money.

'You could have a pickled onion,' Maggie said, the ones she meant were the size of apples and eye-wateringly strong. 'Go on, Stan, dare you.'

'I might, but—'

The bomb cut him off. There wasn't a warning siren. They didn't even hear the plane. The sizzling white flash came out of nowhere.

When Stan opened his eyes again he was lying down, staring up at someone's washing line. It was dark. He was in a back garden. Damp from the grass was soaking into his shorts. The air smelled smoky, like bonfire night but bitter. In the distance, a fire engine wailed.

Stan sat up, dazed. 'June? Maggie?'

There was no sign of his sisters. All he could see was things burning. Pavilion Street, which usually buzzed with buses or grocery vans, or women in aprons chatting over their front gates, was eerily quiet. It felt like he was looking at the world through very thick glass. Where earlier there'd been a row of houses, now he could see straight across to the other side of the street. If this was a dream, then it was a pretty weird one. He wished someone would tell him to wake up.

Stan's legs, at least, were still working. As he got to his feet, string, pennies, a tiny glass bottle he'd found in the deepest part of the river, all tumbled from his torn-to-shreds pockets. Mum would be cross; she was forever mending his clothes.

4

She didn't like him swimming in the river, either. If he wasn't careful, she warned him, the river weed would pull him under and he'd never come up again.

'I'm a decent swimmer,' he'd tried to tell her. 'Better than June, at any rate.'

But his mum was a prize worrier. There'd been another child between June and Stan, who'd died of diphtheria. Though he'd never met Donnie, Stan thought he might've been born to make up for it, which in June's eyes he felt he never would.

Stan began to get his bearings. Behind him was the alley. To his right was their garden gate, still upright, still making that annoying squeak as he pushed it open. Beyond the gate things got confusing again. Stan's legs began to shake, almost as if his body knew before his brain did, because he was still trying to work out where their house had gone. Where it should've been the ground was all caved in. Sticking out on either side of the hole, like the ribs of a long-dead giant animal, were roof timbers from the neighbouring houses.

He'd seen enough blown-apart buildings to be almost numb to it. Amongst the kids on their street, the craze for shrapnel meant scrambling over still-warm bomb sites to get the best bits. Most was from our own anti-aircraft guns. But the bits with German writing on were worth a mint, and June, who liked to be best at everything, had a shoebox full under her bed.

This was *their* house, though. The trembling in Stan's legs spread up his body. All he recognised was their cooker and the bathtub, blown halfway across the yard.

'Mum?' He clung to the hope she'd shout down the stairs, asking him why he'd been out so late. Trouble was the staircase, like the rest of the house, had gone.

Hearing something behind him, he spun round. Two people – one tall, one small – their faces badger-streaked with mud, drifted across the garden towards him. June was still carrying Mum's purse, though he couldn't remember why she had it. Maggie, a few steps behind her, looked stunned.

Stan was so choked with relief, he started to cry. And then he felt ashamed to be the only one blubbing: wasn't that always the way? June never cried at anything. And Maggie was only six, so that didn't really count.

Clumsily, he took his younger sister's hand. 'Are you all right? Is Mum with you?'

'Don't be stupid, Stan, you know she's not!' June snapped.

But he didn't know, and the way June said it made it seem as if he should.

'Where is she, then?' he asked.

'Inside. Too sick to cook our tea, that's where!'

It came back to him in an agonising jolt: Mum bent double coughing, shivering with the flu despite the good weather. Mum getting her coat on, finding her purse, and coughing, coughing. He offered to fetch the chips himself, didn't he, and the others said they'd come too.

'You told Mum to go back to bed.' June scowled at him. 'Don't you remember?'

Stan wasn't sure he did.

June pushed past him for the house. When she saw the huge crater, the broken roof, she stopped. Her shoulders went stiff. Her legs crumpled. She sat down on the ground with a bump. His older sister, who never cried at anything, started sobbing angrily.

'Where's Mum?' Maggie wailed. 'I want Mum.'

Holding her hand a little bit tighter, Stan tried not to admit that he wanted Mum too.

Other people were now arriving – the air-raid warden in his ARP hat, a policeman, two ambulance women carrying blankets and a stretcher.

'But the warning siren didn't even go off,' the policeman was saying.

'It was a leftover bomb, that's why,' the warden

explained. 'The pilot'll have been on a raid up north somewhere, and dropped it on the way home to save fuel.'

'He could've waited another mile or two till he was out over the fields,' an ambulance woman replied. She stopped at June and put a blanket around her, passing another to Stan and Maggie. 'Anyone inside?'

Stan nodded, though before he could explain, the other ambulance woman called out, 'Hey, Sheila! Reckon we've got someone!'

'Quick! Bring your torches over here, please!' the blanket lady yelled.

There was a rush of people, lights, men with buckets, shovels, ropes. Someone was shouting and waving their arms. Maggie lunged forwards.

'Stay back,' Stan warned her, terrified in case they'd found Mum. More terrified that they hadn't.

In the confusion of torch beams and shouting, he thought he glimpsed a hand, an arm, what looked like Mum's bobbly old blue sweater. It was too dark to be sure. June was on her feet, craning to see. Stan couldn't bear to and turned away.

It was the ambulance driver who made him turn back again. She was talking to someone – not urgent or shouty, but like she was sat at the kitchen table, enjoying a cup of tea with a pal.

'Don't worry, love. We'll have you out of there and tucked up in bed in no time.'

She was holding someone's hand. Someone in a blue sweater.

'Mum!' Now Stan was the one rushing forwards.

June grabbed his arm. 'Keep back!'

'Is she all right?' he wanted to know.

'She's alive, at least,' June said, still sounding cross. 'Let them dig her out and get her into the ambulance. You've poked your nose in enough.'

He stared at her. 'Why? What've I done?'

'Mum would've come with us to the chippy if you hadn't been such a fusspot,' June said spitefully.

'Now hang on a minute!' Stan cried. All he'd done was suggest Mum would be better off going back to bed. Besides, like the policeman said, there hadn't even been an air-raid warning. It was unfair to blame everything on him.

2

The next morning, in bright summer sunlight, the damage to Pavilion Street looked worse. Four houses gone in a finger-snap, five more with their roofs staved in. The street was strewn with unexpectedly personal things – a tea caddy, someone's comic, darned grey socks, an egg cup with the name 'Maud' on the front. It made Stan feel lost. What was left of Pavilion Street no longer seemed like home.

Along with the other people whose houses had been bombed, they'd spent the night at the church hall. Fusty-smelling blankets were given out, cups of tea made with milk powder that floated on the top in lumps. The mood was quiet, sombre. Every now and again you'd hear someone snivelling or giving an epic sigh. Though Maggie had fallen asleep quickly, Stan couldn't get comfortable in his spot on the floor. At least their mum was now safe in a hospital bed, though it didn't stop him feeling guilty. What June had said kept going round and round in his head.

He was a fusspot. A worrier like their mum – that's what June thought. Compared to her, maybe he was. His sister had a knack for being annoyingly right.

*

Mid-morning, when the news came that the children of Pavilion Street were being sent to the countryside, Stan was almost relieved. He'd hated saying goodbye to Mum last night as she went off in the ambulance. This stupid war was going on far too long. He was sick of bombs. Sick of air raids and shelters, and not knowing what was going to fall out of the sky next.

He knew most of the other kids in the church hall, at least by sight. Like Lalit Gupta, who lived across the road and was decent with a cricket bat, and Clive Spencer and Tommy Cooke from June's class at school.

'Quiet, children! Quiet, please!' A lady called Mrs Cartwright from the Women's Voluntary Service tried to address them all. 'If you'll just stop talking for a moment—'

Stan felt a bit sorry for her because no one was listening. It was June who finally stood up and yelled, 'SHUT YOUR GOBS, EVERYONE!'

It worked. Now the room was quiet, Mrs Cartwright explained where they were going. She mentioned a bus ride, hills, an old country house. It sounded quite a long way from the city, but Stan tried to think of all the fields there'd be for running in, trees for climbing, and hopefully a river where they could swim.

'Exciting, isn't it, Maggot?' he whispered to Maggie, who was listening with her mouth open.

Clive Spencer didn't think so.

'The Somerset hills?' He pulled a face. 'Not being funny, Mrs Cartwright, but it doesn't sound much of a laugh.'

June hated Clive Spencer. Called him a show-off and a big mouth, which was actually what *she* could be like sometimes. Her mood hadn't improved much this morning, either. Stan felt he was tiptoeing over eggshells.

'It's very kind of Miss Barrington to put us up, Clive,' Mrs Cartwright said patiently. 'There aren't many places able to house twenty children at such short notice.'

Lalit put up his hand. 'I expect the army made her take us, miss. If her house is that big, she has to. It's called requisitioning.'

Mrs Cartwright sighed as if she knew all this, but Stan didn't. And to his surprise he found himself agreeing with Clive Spencer. If they were going miles from home to stay with someone who didn't want them, then it didn't sound so exciting after all.

*

On the map Mrs Cartwright showed them, it looked about seventy miles from Bristol. They set off just after lunch. The bus was slow and hot, with seats that your legs stuck to and windows that didn't open properly. Maggie leaned sleepily against Stan's shoulder. June sat behind them, her knees digging into the back of his seat.

'Don't know why she's still got a grump on,' he muttered to Maggie. He'd hoped going somewhere different might cheer her up.

June nudged his seat. 'Oi! Watch it.'

Stan turned around. 'It's true. You *are* grumpy.'

'Leave me alone,' June said sulkily.

'Don't be cross, Junie.' Maggie yawned.

June glared at her, then at Stan. 'And don't start crying, either. It's about time you toughened up. There's a war on, you know.'

'I *do* know, actually!' Stan replied, frustrated because yet again June was right, he was on the verge of tears.

13

*

By the time the bus reached Taunton, it was making a nasty grinding sound.

'It's not much further!' Mrs Cartwright informed them cheerfully.

But as they left the town behind, and the roads got steeper and narrower, the grinding became a clanking. Steam started to drift past the windows. With lots of revving they got as far as the very top of a hill before the driver stopped. Up ahead the road dipped down sharply to a village.

'It's as far as I'm taking you,' the driver stated. 'You're better off walking from here.'

There were groans, especially from the lucky few who'd salvaged enough from home to have suitcases stuffed with belongings. All that most of the children had with them were the emergency paper bags given by the Red Cross before they'd left Bristol, each with a toothbrush, a flannel and a comb inside. Maggie had been very excited by hers.

Climbing from the bus, they waited to be told what to do next. Stan could feel the sun on the back of his neck. The afternoon was a hot one. He had fond thoughts of cold orange squash, ices, the shady bit in their back garden where he'd play dolls with Maggie when it got too warm to do anything else.

'Is the house we're going to in the village?' Maggie asked, rubbing sleep from her eyes.

''Spect so,' he replied.

As far as Stan could tell there weren't any houses up here, just more very high hedges. There weren't any woods, either, and there definitely wasn't anywhere good for swimming. It all looked rather dull. Not like Pavilion Street with its shops, houses, blocks of flats, church hall, pub, and just a short walk away, his beloved spot where the river ran slow and deep by the railway bridge. Homesickness came over him in a wave. Already the bus was leaving, reversing in a cloud of black smoke up the lane. There was no going back now. Even if they had somewhere to go back *to*.

'This way, please! Hurry up now, no dawdling!' Mrs Cartwright beckoned for the children to follow. Stan kept a wary distance from June.

Instead of heading straight down the hill towards the village, Mrs Cartwright bore right along a narrower lane, down the middle of which grass was growing. The hedges on either side were so tall it was impossible to see over them. It felt like they were walking down a long green tunnel.

'Cripes,' Clive Spencer groaned. 'Talk about the back of beyond!'

Immediately, Clive and Tommy started clowning about, threatening to shove each other into the hedge. When they got bored of that, Clive pushed Tommy into June. It caught her off guard. Made her almost lose her step.

'Are you all right?' Stan was quick to ask.

'Stop *fussing*,' she hissed, then louder so Clive and Tommy would hear, 'What a pair of idiots!'

No one pushed his sister and got away with it. When Stan hadn't been looking, she'd already scooped up a handful of dirt, shaping it in her hand until it was as hard as a stone. June wasn't scared of anything, or anyone. Yet though Stan admired her for it, it made him anxious too. Just as she was about to take aim, Mrs Cartwright halted the group at what appeared to be the entrance to a house.

'Here we are, then!' She clapped her hands for everyone's attention.

With a shiver, Stan stared up at the gates towering above him. They were easily ten feet high, all swirly and dramatic-looking and made of so much iron, it was a wonder they hadn't been taken off to be made into weapons like the local park railings back at home. The gates were shut, not locked. When Mrs Cartwright told them to, the older boys heaved them open.

'Right, children!' she said, in a shrill voice that made her sound nervous. 'Walk in pairs, please. No running, no pushing, Clive and Tommy. And make sure you keep to the drive.'

June took Maggie's hand, so Stan fell in beside Lalit. The driveway they were walking down was flat at first, with trees on either side that made it shady and quite cool.

'Looks an impressive place,' Lalit observed.

Stan wasn't feeling at all enthusiastic. But guessing Lalit was only trying to be friendly, he replied, 'I suppose so – if those gates are anything to go by.'

Rounding a corner, the drive dropped away. Mrs Cartwright called for everyone to halt to admire the view. Stan shielded his eyes against the sun, for he suddenly seemed to be staring right into it.

They were on the edge of a steep valley. At the bottom of it was a house, an enormous sprawling place, with row upon row of huge windows glinting gold in the sunlight.

'Crumbs!' he muttered to Lalit. 'You're right – it *is* impressive!'

Astonishment spread quickly through the group, with cries of 'Wow!' and 'Blimey!' and Clive Spencer telling everyone the house was really a castle.

'No, dear me, it's not a *castle*.' Mrs Cartwright shook her head, then with a proud flourish, explained, 'This is your new home. Frost Hollow Hall.'

Stan didn't know what to make of it. The house looked nothing like 'home' to him. It didn't look remotely frosty, either, sitting in the valley bathed in hot sunshine. He remembered what Lalit had said about requisitioning. The lady who lived here *had* to take them in: it was the law, not a friendly invitation.

All around the house were gardens, the posh kind, with hedges cut into shapes and trees growing in impossibly straight lines. Beyond them, something else sparkled in the sunlight. Stan stood on tiptoe for a better look.

'That's *water*, isn't it?' he asked, all of a sudden interested. 'It is! It's a lake or something!'

'It's a big one. Look how far it goes.' Lalit pointed way beyond the trees, to where the water stretched almost to the valley's edge. It was a proper lake, not like the pond in the park at home where they sailed paper boats sometimes, and the water only reached their knees.

Already Stan was imagining swimming in it. The lake would be ice-cold and clear, and so deep you could dive down for ages and still not reach the bottom. He couldn't wait to give it a try.

Excited now, he nudged Lalit. 'Fancy a dip later?'

Lalit mimed a shudder.

'Don't you swim?' Stan asked. He'd assumed someone good at sport like Lalit would be a strong swimmer too.

'A little.' Lalit waggled his hand. 'But deep water can be very dangerous, my friend. You never know what's underneath.'

'That's what my sister says,' Stan admitted.

Talking of June, he was surprised to see her discussing something with Clive. She still didn't look happy.

'Bet you wouldn't,' Clive said. It sounded as if he was daring her to do something.

'Bet I would.' She didn't look at him, though; she too was staring at the lake as if hypnotised.

3

On the front steps of Frost Hollow Hall, a woman in tweeds greeted them.

'Aha!' she exclaimed. 'Our invaders have arrived!'

Which made them sound like the enemy, Stan thought grimly, even though the woman herself was smiling. Twisting around her ankles in one squirming, yapping mass were so many little sausage dogs that it was impossible to count them.

Stan hung back. He wasn't a great fan of dogs, especially little ones. June had been bitten by one once, and he never forgot how much she'd said it'd hurt.

'That woman looks bonkers. Who *is* she?' Lalit whispered.

'Miss Barrington, the owner, I think,' Stan whispered back. He'd expected someone young like Mum, but the woman had bobbed grey hair and wore a gentleman's suit, which must've been stifling in the heat.

When the woman introduced herself, she was in fact

Miss Potter, the housekeeper. Along with the dogs, who were now licking the children's dusty shoes, it added to the general air of confusion.

'Go on inside, that's right. Don't cause a log jam!' she told them bossily. Thinking her rather terrifying, Stan hurried past.

They found themselves in an entrance hall that was easily the size of a ballroom, and full of people carrying army-issue blankets, bed frames, piles of starched white sheets. It was a job to know where to stand and not be in the way. Though the army had clearly taken over, there was plenty of the old house still to stare at. The walls were full of paintings of men on snorting horses and women wearing floppy hats. Chandeliers dripped light from the ceiling. A huge dark-wood staircase disappeared up to the floor above.

'Does the king live here?' Maggie asked, wide-eyed.

She had a point: Frost Hollow Hall *was* like a palace. Even the floor they were currently standing on was polished marble, which would be superb for skidding across in your socks. Stan's gloomy feeling began to lift again. Perhaps being here wouldn't be too bad. What with the lake outside, and the house being so splendid and grand and old, maybe he'd have an adventure here.

As they waited, not sure what to do next, a woman

stopped to speak to Miss Potter. She had untidy grey hair that was coming loose from its bun, and she looked too old to be lugging things upstairs.

'Where are we putting the boys, Edith?' she asked, pushing strands of hair back with her arm.

'Master Kit's room,' Miss Potter replied.

The older woman's arm went still.

'That's all right, is it, Mum?' Miss Potter added hastily.

''Course 'tis, lovey.' The woman finished tidying her hair and picked up her buckets again. Stan could see the likeness then. Though the mother was skinny where her daughter was stout, they both had the same lively dark eyes. 'It'll do the room good to have a bit of life in it, won't it, eh?'

It left Stan wondering who Master Kit was, and why his bedroom was empty. He glanced again at the portraits on the walls – family pictures, he supposed, of people who'd lived here a very long time ago. *And died here*, he thought uneasily.

*

When their bedrooms were finally ready, the children were taken upstairs. The house was less grand up here, with dusty dark furniture and worn patches in the carpet. Around some of the windows the wallpaper was peeling off.

The wild-haired old woman, who Stan guessed must be called *Mrs* Potter, led them down a corridor full of doors until she stopped at what seemed to be the front of the house. 'Girls on the left, lads on the right,' she said. She had a thick country accent, soft round the edges.

Behind her, Stan glimpsed a stupidly large room in which were rows of narrow hospital-type beds. Out of nowhere, he thought of Mum, all bandaged up and bruised. As the other boys charged in to claim their beds, he hung back, biting his lip. The need to cry suddenly overwhelmed him.

Stuff adventures. Stuff swimming in the lake. He didn't want to be here, sleeping in a room with boys he hardly knew. Right at that moment, he'd rather have shared with his sisters, though they'd gone off quite cheerfully with the other girls. Even June had looked slightly less sour.

Stan sniffed back his tears, unaware that Mrs Potter was still in the corridor.

'The first night away from home's always tough,' she said, making him jump. 'A kind person told me that, many years ago.'

'I'll survive.' He quickly dabbed his eyes with his shirtsleeve.

She smiled. ''Course you will. I was about your age, you know, when I went away from home. I didn't have nobody with me that first night, but I soon made a good friend. You've got a head start though, son. Some of your family are here with you, aren't they?'

He didn't mean to snort. 'Fat lot of help that is, Mrs Potter. My big sister bloomin' well hates me!'

'Pah!' Her eyes went skywards. 'Sisters, eh? Well, I ain't spoken to mine for over sixty years!'

Stan was amazed. He couldn't imagine any argument lasting that long.

'She took off to America with my pa – stole him away from me, more like, when I was always his favourite,' Mrs Potter said. 'Never came back home again, neither.'

She wasn't laughing any more. She looked almost sad, or angry, or a mix of both.

'I'm sorry to trouble you,' Stan muttered. 'I'm not usually a crybaby.'

Mrs Potter patted his arm. 'Daft, in't it? Everyone expects boys to be strong and brave, but in my experience, they're far more likeable when they're honest about what they're feeling.' She sighed. 'So, as we've shared a few confidences, you'd better call me Tilly.'

'I'm Stanley,' he replied. 'You can call me Stan.'

He liked Tilly. She had a sparky, cheeky glint in her eye, like maybe she'd been a bit of a mischief-maker in her day. He betted she wouldn't be afraid to tackle a German if she ever saw one.

'Frost Hollow Hall is a fine old house. Belongs to a fine old family too,' Tilly told him. 'You'll settle in soon enough.'

'Best thing I've seen so far is the lake,' Stan ventured.

Tilly's face changed.

'Can't we go in it?' he asked, wondering if he'd said the wrong thing. 'I'm a really good swimmer, and can hold my breath underwater for nearly—'

'No,' Tilly interrupted sharply. 'You can't.'

'Why not, though? It's baking hot today, and swimming's such a jolly good way to cool off.'

Tilly narrowed her eyes like she was considering how best to answer. 'Places have memories, young man,' she said eventually. 'That lake harbours some very bad ones, and they're best left in peace.'

She gave him a clean hankie that smelled of peppermint. 'Dry your eyes properly, there's a good lad. We've seen enough tears at Frost Hollow Hall.'

4

Right from the word go there were leaders amongst the children, and it was no surprise to Stan who they were. Early the next day, in the ten minutes after breakfast before lessons started, June called a meeting. Everyone piled into the girls' bedroom, where his sister settled herself cross-legged on her bed. Clive was next to her, leaning on the bedside table. They had the look of a king and queen, if you ignored June's turned-away shoulder and Clive's smirking face. Stan could see it was an uneasy sort of truce.

'If this place is going to be our home like Miss Potter says,' June told them, 'then there shouldn't be so many stupid rules.'

She was referring to the moment at breakfast when Miss Potter had stood up, tapping her teacup for quiet. Everyone stopped talking but carried on eating so all you could hear was the sloshy sound of twenty sets of chewing jaws.

'We want Frost Hollow Hall to feel like your home.'
Miss Potter's smile was tight. 'But please bear in mind
it is our home as well, and so parts of the property will
remain out of bounds to you.'

Which immediately got everyone listening a bit
harder.

'Firstly, no passing through the green baize doors to
the servants' quarters. Secondly,' she ticked the places
off on her fingers, 'stay away from the East Wing of the
house. Those are Miss Barrington's quarters, and let's
just say she wasn't very agreeable to having you here.'

We didn't exactly want *to come either*, Stan thought
to himself.

'The other place you're forbidden,' she went on, her
eyes scanning the room, 'is the lake. It is completely,
utterly out of bounds.'

A blush crept up Stan's face. He'd a sneaking
suspicion this was to do with what he'd told
Tilly yesterday about wanting to go swimming. It
disappointed him that she'd passed on what he'd said,
yet her reaction, and now her daughter's, was pretty
intriguing. There was something about that lake:
something mysterious and strange.

'I know it's summer, and a hot one too. But if I catch
any of you out there, there'll be consequences. Is that

understood?' Miss Potter went on, fiercely enough to get the message across.

As soon as she sat down, Clive started trying to catch Tommy's eye. That was the trouble with him: you told him not to do something, and straight away he'd work out how to.

Which was exactly what was happening here now, in the girls' bedroom.

'So.' Clive took over from where June left off. He rubbed his hands with glee. 'We're going to have a little game.'

Stan's heart sank. Clive's games usually involved hurting someone or smashing up people's stuff. It didn't help that Maggie was listening eagerly, hanging on Clive's every word.

'Here's what we do,' Clive explained. 'All them places we're banned from? We go to each one – the servants' quarters, the East Wing, the lake – and nick something to prove we've been there.'

A hum of excitement spread around the room.

Lalit gave Stan a knowing look. 'I can guess where you'll be going first.'

He didn't reply. He'd wanted to go swimming, that was all. To dive beneath the water and block out the world. But after what Tilly told him yesterday, he sensed something bad had happened out there, that the lake was somehow jinxed. And now that it'd become part of Clive and June's stupid game, it felt well and truly spoiled.

'It'll be a competition,' June added. 'Two teams: boys versus girls. Whichever team gets the most daring things will be the winners.'

'And remember the rules,' Clive told them. 'You absolutely *have* to take something as proof you've done the dare. Otherwise, we'll think you've fibbed.'

A few of the boys flexed their muscles, thinking themselves champions already. But Stan knew all too well that his sister had more nerve than any of them. She'd never let Clive's team win. He wished he was on her side, but as she still wasn't really talking to him – and he was a boy – he supposed he could forget about it.

'What's the prize for winning?' Lalit asked.

'Chocolate?' one of the younger boys suggested hopefully.

'Cake?' Maggie added.

'To go home?' Stan blurted out.

The room went quiet.

'That ain't going to happen.' Clive gave him a withering look. 'So you'd best get used to it.'

29

It was the sort of moment where normally June would step in and tell Clive to leave off teasing her little brother. Today, though, she looked the other way.

*

All morning, they sat through Miss Potter's attempt at a maths lesson. Despite a maid coming in to open all the windows, the room was like a furnace. It made the children sleepy and headachy. Usually Stan was quite quick at sums, but today his brain felt like treacle.

At least no one mentioned the dare game again, and by mid-morning break another bit of news was doing the rounds. One of the younger kids, a red-haired girl called Sadie, said last night she'd woken up to find a woman sitting at the end of her bed.

'What a load of old codswallop!' Clive snorted.

Although close to tears, Sadie stuck to her story. 'I'm not fibbing, honest I'm not. I heard the bed springs squeak when she stood up again. She was real. I saw her.'

All the little kids, Maggie included, looked worried.

'Don't worry, Maggot,' Stan tried to reassure her. 'It was probably just a dream.'

But he wondered if maybe Frost Hollow Hall had a ghost. And from the anxious looks on the other children's faces he could tell he wasn't the only one thinking it.

Lunch was disgusting. Bone soup was its official name, though it looked like greasy dishwater. The only good thing was that there were no more lessons afterwards. Once they were dismissed from the dining hall, they were free to spend the afternoon as they wished.

'Though don't forget what I explained to you this morning,' Miss Potter reminded them.

Clive tapped his nose at June, who folded her arms with a scowl. Stan groaned to himself: by the looks of things, the dare game was still very much on. So it was a bit of a relief when Lalit asked him if he fancied exploring the gardens.

'Sounds like a top plan,' Stan agreed.

Back home, he'd never had much to do with Lalit, who went to a different school on the other side of the city that Mum said was for ridiculously clever students. Stan was glad of him now though: he was easy company, and talked about stuff other than dares and ghosts.

It was hot outside, so they left their school jumpers on the bench in the front porch. Maggie's cardigan was there too – Stan noticed the name tag sewn inside. He'd not seen her at lunch, he realised then.

'I'll catch up with you in a minute,' he told Lalit. 'I just want to check Maggie's all right.'

He found her almost straight away on the upstairs landing.

'There you are!' he said. 'Aren't you hungry? You missed lunch.'

Instead of answering, Maggie beckoned him to come closer. He'd noticed by now that she was wearing someone else's school jumper: it was so big it reached to her knees. What's more, there seemed to be something hidden inside it. Something that was moving.

'What are you up to?' Stan asked.

'I've done the dare thing!' she whispered. 'Look! I've got Lobelia!'

He frowned. '*Who?*'

'It says on her collar, look.'

Before she could show him, a sausage dog stuck her head out to see what was happening. Unlike the others Stan had seen, this one had a rough coat. Her little whiskery head made her look like an otter.

'Oh, you haven't!' Stan gulped. 'Miss Potter'll go mad!'

He wasn't sure if he was impressed or horrified. The dog, though, was actually rather sweet, and he gave her a tentative stroke.

'She's not Miss Potter's,' Maggie told him. 'I got her from that east place, down there.' She pointed back down the stairs into the hall where, in a dark corner, was the door to the East Wing. 'It wasn't very nice, either. Not like out here. The lamps were funny old ones, and it was dark and rather creepy.'

'You went to the *East Wing*?'

'Yes. There was a woman in there, asleep in a chair.'

'Was it Miss Potter?'

Maggie shook her head. 'She had a nice face, though. Lobelia was curled up on her lap.'

He stared at Maggie. Never mind that he didn't think much of this daft game, or that being a boy meant he wasn't even on his sister's team. The woman Maggie had just stumbled across was probably Miss Barrington, the actual owner of Frost Hollow Hall. She was the only person he knew of who lived in the East Wing of the house. And to have scooped up the dog asleep on her lap, well, that was a seriously impressive dare.

'Wowzers, Maggot! Good work!' he gasped.

Maggie beamed.

'You'd better go and show June, I suppose,' he added reluctantly.

Lobelia had other plans. A sudden wriggle and she was out of Maggie's arms, racing down the stairs.

5

To make matters worse, the front door was wide open. Though Stan and Maggie flew after her, the little sausage dog was too quick, bolting straight outside into the sunshine. By the time they reached the front steps, there was no sign of her anywhere.

'Great.' Stan ran a hand through his hair. 'Now what?'

Maggie's bottom lip started to tremble.

'No crying, Maggot,' he warned her.

'But if I haven't got Lobelia then my dare won't even count,' she wailed. 'We have to have proof. Clive said so.'

And Clive's a chump, thought Stan angrily.

The gardens were huge. To the left were lawns, to the right trees, hedges, flower beds full of roses and wildflowers. And after that, a path leading to a wicket gate and the woods beyond. Finding a small dog out here would be like searching for a dropped penny on a pebble beach.

Yet suddenly Maggie yelled, 'There she is!'

Sure enough, about a hundred yards away, darting between the hedges, was a small brown shape. Maggie jumped up and down. 'Lobelia! Coooo-eeee! Come here, good girl!'

Though the shouts practically deafened Stan, Lobelia ignored them. They quickly lost sight of her again. Stan tried not to think about Miss Barrington waking up to find her dog missing. Or that when he finally caught the little rat, he'd have to pick her up somehow. He really didn't have Maggie's confidence with animals.

Meanwhile, the sound of yelling had brought Lalit back across the lawn to the house. He was carrying what appeared to be a croquet mallet.

'I was coming to ask if you wanted a game,' he said.

'My sister will,' Stan replied quickly before Maggie could object. 'Just don't let her do any more dares.'

Following Lobelia's trail was relatively easy. Being so stumpy and low to the ground, she flattened the grass with her belly as she went. Very soon she was back in Stan's sights, but by heck, she could move. Running as fast as he could, Stan still didn't stand a chance of catching her.

'Come here, you little worm!' he cried, wiping the sweat from his face.

The more he shouted the more Lobelia thought it all a wonderful game. She even had the cheek to stop every so often, wag her tail, then, just as he made a grab for her, bound off across the garden. It was so frustrating.

Stan would've given up there and then if it wasn't for Maggie. He'd already disappointed one sister: he wasn't about to let the other one down. Besides, Being outwitted by a sausage dog wasn't a thing to be proud of.

Having done a good few laps of the garden, he now – rather gratefully – found himself in a cool, shady spot surrounded by hedges. They were the tall, clipped kind that rose up like dark green walls, and seemed to soak up noise. The air, for being so still, felt softer too. The dog had disappeared again.

Stan walked on, trailing his fingers over the leaves. Up ahead, the hedges forked, one path veering left, the other curving to the right. He wasn't sure which way to go. Lobelia's belly-tracks had long since disappeared, so perhaps it would be a better idea to go back the way he came. But when he turned around, the hedges looked different. There were other hidden paths he'd not noticed before, and the hedges themselves seemed to block out the light. If this was one of those garden mazes, then he was lost.

The only thing for it was to keep walking. Stan turned back, sticking to the path he was on and following it to the right. He prayed he'd find Lobelia up ahead.

Rounding the corner, he stopped.

'Woweee!' Stan stepped back and gazed upwards.

It wasn't the dog he'd found but an enormous statue of an angel. He'd seen similar ones in church graveyards, all floaty-looking with big feathery wings. Only this one was so huge, he had to tip his head right back to take it all in.

The grave, so the writing on it said, was Christopher Edward Barrington's, known as Kit. He'd died in 1871. With that surname, he had to be a relative of *Miss* Barrington. And, Stan guessed, probably the same Master Kit in whose bedroom the boys slept.

Reading the dates beneath the name, he did a quick bit of maths. Poor Kit had only been fifteen when he died, nearly the same age as June. It was hard to imagine her – loud, full of life, annoying – being dead.

The quiet between the hedges felt eerie, suddenly. Gooseflesh spread up Stan's arms. The stone angel stared down at him, blank-eyed and yet at the same time as if it could see right inside him.

'Stuff this for a lark,' Stan muttered to himself.

Hurrying in what he hoped was the direction of the house, he found the right way surprisingly quickly. It was a joy to be out in the warmth again, to feel the sun on his face.

Passing the flower beds, he heard a snuffling behind him.

'There you are, you toerag!' he cried, as Lobelia trotted past like butter wouldn't melt.

This time he managed to grab her.

'Don't you dare bite me,' he warned, holding her at arm's length.

She wagged her tail, wriggling furiously like a caught fish until she managed to land a lick on his nose. It tickled, making him laugh.

'All right, all right,' he said, cradling her like he'd seen Maggie do. As Lobelia closed her eyes blissfully, even Stan could see she was about as savage as a baby mouse.

On the lawn, he found Lalit playing croquet alone.

'What on earth have you got there?' he cried.

'Miss Barrington's dog: my little sister's contribution to the dare game. Where is she, by the way?'

'She went off with your other sister,' Lalit replied. 'The bossy one.'

Stan grimaced. 'Thanks. I'd better go and find them.'

Almost immediately, back at the house, he ran into June. She was sitting on the stairs, combing her hair. Maggie was nowhere to be seen.

'Where's Maggot?' he asked.

'Upset,' June replied. 'Something about a dog she says she got from the East Wing, but it ran away and now no one will believe her.' Then her eyes snagged on Lobelia. 'Thought you didn't like dogs.'

'This one's quite nice, actually,' Stan admitted.

She laughed. It wasn't a nice laugh, either. 'Oh, I get it. That's *the* dog, isn't it? The one Maggot's upset about?'

'She's called Lobelia,' Stan tried to explain. 'And she's a right little—'

June interrupted. 'You're going to take her straight to Clive, aren't you?'

'Why would I do that? It's Miss Barrington's dog, not his.'

June rolled her eyes irritably. 'Because of the game. You've found Maggot's dog and now you're going to claim the dare for your team.'

'No, I'm not!' Stan didn't like how she was twisting things around.

'Good.' June resumed her hair-combing. 'You

wouldn't want to choose Clive Spencer over your own sisters, would you?'

'Actually, I'd be on your team if you'd let me.'

'You're a boy, Stan. That's not how it works.'

'But I'm your family,' he told her. 'And we don't have to tell anyone.'

He felt stupid, pleading with his own sister. But to his surprise she put down her comb.

'I s'pose we could …' She sucked in her cheeks, thinking it over. 'Tell you what, I'll give you a trial. But you'll have to do the dares.'

'I will,' he replied, a bit too eagerly.

'And you promise to be brave?'

'Promise.'

'Because we're going to win this game,' she warned him. 'We're going to wipe that smug look off Clive Spencer's face and stuff it in his back pocket.'

It might have been a threat, or a truce. Only time would tell. In the meantime, June insisted he hand over Lobelia as proof of Maggie's dare.

*

At supper, Clive was so unnaturally quiet Miss Potter asked him if he was sick.

'The score's one–nil to us,' June whispered to Stan, which explained it. 'Don't get too excited, though,' she warned him. 'There's still two more dares to go.'

6

That night Stan awoke with a start. Through gaps in the curtains, moonlight shone in, and as his eyes adjusted to the dark, he was able to make out the other boys' beds. They were arranged in three rows of four, the best spot being near the window where Clive and his chums slept. At that moment, he was glad not to be on his own. His earlier encounter with Kit Barrington's grave had spooked him. Not to mention what Sadie had told them about her strange night-time visitor. But now he had promised June he'd be brave, he'd have to start acting it. Easier said than done.

As he rolled over in bed, Stan felt the wet patch.

'Oh no!' he muttered.

There was no mistaking the cold clammy sheets or his soggy pyjama trousers. Being in a room with eleven other boys didn't feel so reassuring, suddenly. He couldn't bear it if any of them found out he'd wet the bed.

As quietly as he could, Stan untucked the top and bottom sheet, and peeled off his trousers. Over by the window, Tommy turned over in bed. Stan froze. Once he'd started snoring again, Stan yanked on his school shorts, grabbed the wet sheets and legged it out of the room. He stopped at the top of the stairs to think. All he had to do was find where the clean sheets were kept and dump the wet lot in the laundry. It couldn't be that difficult.

Stan crept down the stairs to the hallway. Despite it being a warm night, he felt suddenly rather cold. A prickling sensation came over him, as if he was being watched. Sadie's story flared up in his brain again but he pushed it aside, remembering his promise to June.

In the dark the door to the servants' quarters looked the same as all the others, but felt fuzzy to the touch, like it was covered in carpet. The door opened on to stone steps, which led to a passageway. Stan took a deep breath. He wasn't scared, exactly. He just wished he'd brought a torch.

Down in the servants' quarters, the only light came from little high-up windows. Ahead of him, all along the passage, moonlight fell in silver patches on the floor. Stan took it as a sign – a reassuring one – that he was heading in the right direction for the linen cupboard.

The first room he came to was the kitchen. He'd never seen so many pots and pans in one place, nor a dresser so big it covered the entire wall. It'd take a whole army to run a kitchen like this. And all just for Miss Barrington.

June said she'd never want to be a maid. No young person in their right mind did these days, apparently. Better jobs were to be had in shops or factories, which was why so many big old houses were being divided up into flats or knocked down completely. Sad when you thought about it.

Through a pair of glass doors, the passage went on. And on. A whole other house seemed to exist down here, one that was bare and practical, like the engine of a giant machine. Stan started to worry he'd get lost again. The wet sheets, bundled up against his chest, smelled unpleasant. He needed to find a washtub and a linen cupboard – and get a wriggle on too.

Thankfully, a few doors down he found the laundry room. In it was a sink, an enormous mangle, and what looked to be an old copper for doing the wash in. On the floor were buckets: filling one with water, Stan stuffed the sheets and pyjama trousers in to soak. It was a relief to be rid of them. Now all he had to do was find some clean bedclothes.

Out in the passage, the moon had lost its brightness, making it hard to see anything but the dark shapes of doorways and the grey stone floor. Stan could almost feel the weight of the house's thick old walls pressing in on him. Despite his best efforts, he was soon thinking about 'ghosts' again. It wasn't exactly hard to, down here, on his own. He told himself not to be a chicken. In old houses like this someone was bound to have died over the years – Kit Barrington had. It didn't mean Frost Hollow Hall was haunted.

The corridor came to an abrupt halt. Two cupboards faced him, which looked as promising for storing laundry as anywhere had. Inside the first were pails and fusty-smelling floor mops. It took a good heave on the handle to open the other. The smell coming from inside was damp, old – a bit like this whole house smelled – only strong enough to catch in Stan's throat. Stacked inside the cupboard were boxes, a fair few of them too. Disappointed not to find any sheets, he was about to shut the door when he noticed the top box wasn't properly shut. Something gleamed inside.

Reaching into the packing straw, he felt books, a biscuit tin, and then something cold, like metal. Stan lifted it from the box. It seemed to be an ice skate, the leather old and dry, the blade rough with rust. The boot was for a largish left foot. Checking the box again, he couldn't find the other boot to make up the pair.

That didn't much matter, though. He was suddenly thinking of the dare. If he gave June the skate, it'd be proof that he'd been down here, in the servants' quarters. He didn't have to be completely honest about what he'd *actually* been looking for. As far as he knew, no one else had gone below stairs yet, especially not in the dead of night. It'd put them ahead in the game, two–nil. It was too good an opportunity to miss.

Forgetting sheets, he stuffed the skate inside his pyjama shirt and hurried back to the green baize door. He was almost at the top of the steps when he heard a thumping noise, then voices in the hallway. The dogs started barking. Footsteps tap-tapped across the marble floor.

'I don't know who it is, Sylvia, so stop clinging on to my arm.' The voice was Miss Potter's. 'The only way we'll find out is by opening the door.'

7

Bang bang bang!

Stan cowered as a light flickered under the door. Thankfully, they weren't coming for him. The door Miss Potter was talking about was the *front* door. Someone was hammering on it mightily hard too. The dogs' barking had turned into a manic, high-pitched shrieking.

Stan opened the servants' door a tiny crack, pressing his eye up against it to see what was happening. The lamps were all on. The hallway looked grand and impressive, and not remotely haunted any more.

Miss Potter was now standing on the doorstep.

'What the devil do you want at this hour?' she cried. For all her bluster, Stan could hear the wobble in her voice.

'Sylvia' hovered behind, thin and nervous in her dressing gown. He guessed she was the famous Miss Barrington, since in her arms, squirming to get down, was Lobelia.

Please don't let it be spies out there, or Nazis, Stan thought, excitement *and* terror making his heart thud. Old Tilly might be able to see off a German, but he couldn't imagine these two or their sausage dogs putting up much of a fight.

Miss Potter's tone changed to one of surprise. 'Oh! We've got a bit of a situation, have we? You'd better come in, then, all of you. Chop chop!'

Within moments the hallway was full of soldiers, around whose ankles the dogs were now wriggling and whimpering for attention. Though Stan only counted about fifteen men, they were as solid and as broad as oak trees, and wearing smart beige-coloured uniforms with funny hats that sat on their heads at a crazy angle. As if to make the point, the man in charge took his off very politely.

'Ma'am,' he said, in a deep drawling voice, 'forgive us for intruding on you in the dead of night.'

'Good grief, American soldiers!' gasped Miss Barrington, clutching her dressing gown to her throat.

Stan's eyes were on stalks. He'd only ever seen Americans on the cinema screen and loved how they always knew the right thing to do. He loved the accent too, and hearing it out in the hallway now made Miss Barrington's proper cut glass way of speaking sound as if she should be a presenter on the radio.

He eased the door open a fraction more.

'Ma'am,' the man in charge said again, 'my name is Colonel Bagatelli.' He had dark, slicked-back hair and a moustache so thin someone could've drawn it on with a pen. 'I'm afraid our driver here, Johnson ...' he thumbed at the person standing rather guiltily behind him, 'he took a wrong turn on the main road, and now our truck is stuck in a ditch, just outside your gates.'

'Oh dear,' Miss Barrington gasped. 'No one's hurt, I hope?'

'No, ma'am, though the truck's leaking oil and is gonna need fixing.'

'My father has a farm horse. He can pull your truck out—' Miss Potter began.

'Tomorrow, Edith,' Miss Barrington interrupted, then smiled at Colonel Bagatelli. To be fair, he was movie-star handsome, and it was clear as day that she'd noticed. 'You're welcome to stay here tonight.'

'Thank you, ma'am.' The colonel gave a little bow, then ordered his soldiers to take off their boots. They did this in a flash – all except the driver, Johnson, who was gazing up at the paintings and the chandeliers. He was dark-skinned – darker than Lalit – and, like the other soldiers, was muscular, tall and handsome. Yet the way he stared about him, almost damp-eyed with emotion, got Stan thinking about what Tilly had said, about boys showing their feelings.

Bet he's never seen anywhere like this before, either, Stan thought, remembering how he'd been dazzled by the house when he first arrived. Actually, he still was. There was something strange, something magical about Frost Hollow Hall. Something he couldn't quite explain in words. He could feel it, though, like a tingle under his skin.

Meanwhile, as the late-night visitors headed for the library, something caught Miss Potter's eye on the stairs.

'You, girl!' she barked. 'Get back to bed at once!'

Stan cringed: he wasn't meant to be out of bed, either. Pretty soon the Americans would want sandwiches and cocoa, and when Miss Potter went to the kitchens, she'd find him hiding behind the door.

So, once it was safe to do so, he made a break for it and crept out into the hall. From the library came the sounds of chairs being dragged across the floor. On tiptoe, and keeping a tight hold of the ice skate, he sprinted up the stairs. He found June in her nightdress, sitting near the bannister at the top.

'Crikey!' he gasped. 'Was it *you* Miss Potter just shouted at?'

She nodded. 'She saw my feet dangling down.'

June, being June, hadn't gone back to bed as she'd been told to, she'd simply tucked her feet out of sight. In the half-dark of the landing, his sister's face was all hollows and shadows. Her teeth were chattering.

'What's the matter?' he whispered, crouching next to her.

'I know it sounds stupid, but someone was sitting at the bottom of my bed,' she said, frowning. 'I was having a dream about fire, or explosions, or something. The person being there woke me up.'

Stan shivered a little. 'What, like happened to Sadie last night?'

'I think so. I felt her there. She didn't say anything – just sat there, that's all.'

'Was it a woman, then?'

'I reckon so, though I didn't see her. She smelled nice. Sort of flowery.'

It really wasn't like June to make up stuff like this. All over again, Stan began to wonder if the house was haunted. Hadn't Tilly mentioned something about bad memories and tears?

The ice skate, meanwhile, was digging into his ribs.

'I've got something to show you,' Stan said, hoping it would cheer her up.

'Go on, then,' June said, yawning into her hand. 'What is it?'

As soon as she saw the skate she sat up, alert. 'Jeez, Stan! That's awfully old, that is! Where's the other one?'

'I dunno.' Stan was pleased at her reaction. 'The boot's for a left foot, and from the size of it, I'd say it belonged to a man.'

'Let me have a proper look. Where did you find it?'

Stan gave it to her.

'In a cupboard, in the servants' quarters,' he answered. He'd no plans to tell her why he'd been down there in the first place. And luckily, she was too busy inspecting the boot and running her fingers along the blade to notice he was wearing school shorts.

'It's not very sharp,' Stan pointed out.

A slow smile spread across June's face. It was ages since he'd seen her look like that. 'But I bet Clive Spencer hasn't got one. I'd say that's two–nil to us, wouldn't you?'

8

The next morning, Stan overslept. Everyone else was already at breakfast, so at least when he threw back the blankets there was no one there to see his damp, sheetless mattress.

As he took his seat at the table, he sensed he'd just walked in on more good news. Maggie waved to him, beaming. Lalit was laughing and telling awful jokes. The only person not chatting, not grinning from ear to ear, was June, which, come to think of it, wasn't that unusual.

'What've I missed?' Stan asked Lalit, as he prodded a bowl of rubbery porridge.

His friend grinned. 'Can you believe it? Some American soldiers turned up here in the night!'

'Never!' Trying to fake surprise made Stan nearly choke on his breakfast. He was dying to tell Lalit that he'd seen the Americans arrive. And that they were magnificent, like heroes from a comic book, and Miss

Barrington had fallen in love with their colonel. But then he'd have to explain why he'd been hiding behind the baize door, which wasn't a great idea.

'And . . .' Lalit jiggled his knee impatiently, 'they're using the library as their quarters, so we can't have any lessons this morning! Miss Potter's just announced it!'

'Brilliant!' Now that was *proper* good news.

Out in the hallway, the soldiers were on the move. Hearing their accents, the stomp of their boots, Stan put down his spoon. He was too excited to eat.

The front door opened.

'Are they leaving?' Tommy asked.

'They can't be!' Lalit cried. 'Not already!'

And suddenly everyone was on their feet, rushing to the windows for a glimpse of the Americans.

'I can't see!' Maggie squealed, so Stan hoisted her on to his shoulders.

As they waved and whistled, the soldiers waved back. Stan would never have guessed they'd spent the night sleeping in the library in its uncomfortable chairs. They looked bright-eyed and strong, and ready for anything.

In amongst them Stan spotted Johnson, the truck driver. He supposed it must be a bit embarrassing to crash a truck, especially when all your mates were on board. But if Johnson was feeling it, it didn't show. He seemed as cheery and upbeat as every other soldier marching past the front of the house.

'For goodness' sake, children, come away from that window at once!' Miss Potter bellowed. No one took any notice. Tommy gave Clive a leg up so he could open one of the windows.

'Hey!' he shouted to the soldiers. 'Got any gum, chum?'

The Americans laughed, rolling their eyes like they'd heard it all before. But a couple of them, checking their pockets, came right up to the window. It made Stan feel suddenly shy and small.

'There ya go, sonny,' one of the soldiers said. In hands as big as shovels, he held out a dozen or so bits of gum. There were squeals, fingers scrabbling, pushing and jostling. Most people got some before Miss Potter elbowed her way through and slammed the window shut.

'That's quite enough of that,' she said briskly.

Yet once they'd cleared the breakfast things, she did consent to take the children up to the gates to watch the soldiers' truck being pulled from the ditch.

They set off up the drive, a wriggling crocodile of children. Stan was enjoying himself – not that he was a great fan of motor trucks like some of the other boys, but he was fascinated by the Americans. So much so he'd almost forgotten about the lake, and seeing it now as he glanced behind him at the view, the thrill of swimming there stirred him again. It was the last forbidden part of the estate. The final dare in the game. A place full of bad memories that were best left in peace, so Tilly said.

Except, seeing it diamond-bright in the morning sunshine, it looked so tempting. He could almost feel the cool water lapping over his feet, his shins, his shoulders.

'That Clive Spencer is a pain in the neck,' June fumed, catching him up as they walked.

'What's happened now?' Stan asked. He'd thought she'd still be pleased as punch after last night's find.

'He reckons he knows where the other ice skate is. Says he's heard a rumour it's at the bottom of the lake, and he's going to fetch it.'

'Oh, he said so, did he?' Stan sighed: it was a typical Clive Spencer-type brag.

'He did,' June insisted. 'Says he overheard one of the servants talking. He reckons if he can find it then he's won.'

'But that's only one dare. We've won two,' Stan reminded her.

'True, but according to him this is the most difficult dare by far. He says it's worth all the others put together.'

It sounded like Clive was making up the rules as he went along. But Stan could see how determined his sister was: much as he admired her for it, it worried him too.

'I'm not letting him think he's the best,' June stated. 'I'm going to the lake myself, just as soon as I can get away. Give me a few minutes' head start then come after me, will you?'

Stan hesitated. His sister wasn't a particularly good swimmer. She didn't like diving under the water, either. So how on earth did she think she was going to find an ice skate in such an enormous lake?

'Don't go chicken on me, Stan,' she warned. 'I'm counting on you to help.'

So he found himself nodding. He'd be glad when this dare game was over. More than anything, though, he wanted his sister to win.

*

At the gates they met an oldish man leading an enormous chestnut horse.

'You're the Bristol kiddies, are you, eh?' the man asked. He told them he was called Mr Potter, and with his square jaw and mop of thick grey hair he did look like his daughter. Unlike her, though, he smiled a lot. He then introduced his horse, who stood patiently while the soldiers attached ropes to her harness.

'Blimey, she's the size of an elephant,' Tommy Cooke sniggered.

'And she's got a name, son,' Mr Potter said pointedly. 'Gladys. She's a Suffolk Punch, not an elephant, just so you know.'

'That's a breed of horse,' Lalit whispered, seeing Stan looking confused.

Gladys was the biggest, shiniest, most gentle horse Stan had ever met. When Maggie tried to stroke her all she could reach was the horse's shoulder. Even the Americans had to climb on to the gates to fasten the harness across her armchair-wide back.

Once everything was ready, the children were ordered to stand at a safe distance. The truck was a few yards further down the lane, the wheels on its left side wedged in the ditch. The whole thing was at a very dramatic angle. Its right wheels were off the ground, its windscreen smashed. Stan couldn't believe no one had been hurt.

'Whoa!' Lalit breathed in sharply. 'Look at that, would you?' He was pointing behind the truck to the lane beyond. 'A dead straight road. No skid marks in the dirt. Those tyre tracks look like the driver swerved.'

'Maybe a deer jumped out, or a rabbit or something?' Stan offered.

'Maybe.' Lalit shrugged. 'Or maybe it was deliberate.'

'*Deliberate?*' Stan thought it over, but couldn't imagine why Johnson would have caused an accident on purpose.

Any evidence of Lalit's suggestion was lost pretty fast under Gladys's gigantic hooves and the boots of the American soldiers as the ground got churned up, pressed down, scuffed. A few almighty heaves and the truck came free. With a creaky bounce it was back in the lane, all four tyres on the ground. Everyone clapped, whooped. This was far better than a maths lesson any day of the week. Even Miss Potter was smiling. Though you could see from the oil dripping out underneath that the truck wasn't roadworthy yet.

'Easy, good girl.' Mr Potter clapped Gladys's sweating neck.

A circle of kids quickly gathered round, wanting to make a fuss of the horse and chat some more to Mr Potter. Stan looked for June but couldn't see her, so guessed she must've already slipped away. Silently, he started counting down the few minutes' head start he'd promised her.

It was then he realised Johnson was beckoning him over.

'Say, young fella, you fancy showing me where *Mrs* Potter lives?' he said. 'I've something for her.'

Stan stopped counting.

'Tilly, d'you mean?' It was the name he knew Mrs Potter by.

'That's the one,' Johnson confirmed. 'Called Tilly Higgins before she married.'

Stan didn't know about that part of things, and he was surprised that Johnson, an American GI, did. But he'd an idea of where she lived. There were two cottages behind the main house, where he'd seen her going to and fro.

'Can we go, like, *now*?' Johnson sounded urgent. 'I'll cover for you if you get into trouble.'

No one seemed to be looking their way. And because Johnson was so very tall and smart, and super polite, Stan was rather chuffed to have been singled out to help.

'All right,' he said, knowing June would be expecting him at the lake. 'But we'll have to be double quick.'

9

Johnson took such huge great strides Stan had to jog to keep up. By the time they reached the cottages he was sweating. He'd also learned that Johnson's first name was Edward.

'Buddy, you can call me Eddie,' he said, which made Stan like him even more.

The two flint cottages were reached by cutting through the stable yard and going down a cinder path. When Tilly answered the door of the first one they came to, she had a shawl round her shoulders, her hair still plaited for bed. At her feet on the front step was a pile of bridles, halters and ropes.

'Excuse the mess,' she said, tutting. 'My husband couldn't find the right ropes this morning, and he's never one to tidy up after himself. It's him you're after, I take it?'

'No,' Stan panted. 'It's you we want – or rather, Eddie here wants.'

He glanced at Eddie, who'd gone quiet. He'd taken off his funny little army cap and was twisting it nervously in his hands.

'You're one of them Yankees, are you?' Tilly looked him up and down. 'Did my husband and Gladys get your truck out all right?'

'Yes, ma'am, thank you, ma'am,' Eddie mumbled.

'An accident, was it? Or you boys having a lark?' Tilly asked, amused.

'Um ... errr ...' Eddie had gone so tongue-tied all of a sudden, Stan wondered what was the matter with him.

'An accident,' Stan said for him. He didn't honestly think Eddie *had* crashed their truck on purpose. He was pretty sure Lalit had got that wrong.

'I'd best be off,' Stan said now, backing away. 'My sister's waiting for me.'

'Oh?' Tilly's eyebrows shot up. 'Speaking again, are you? Not going for the sixty-year record like me?'

Though she was joking, Eddie looked suddenly even more uncomfortable. Something was going on here, and Stan had no idea what. Now wasn't the time to get caught up in it, either.

'There's a game of dare going on between the boys and the girls, that's all,' he told her.

Tilly tutted again, more crossly this time. 'Don't play dares, that's my advice. It never ends well.'

'It's a bit late for that. Clive Spencer says there's an old ice skate at the bottom of the lake, so we're going to—' Stan stopped, seeing Tilly's face. She looked plain horrified.

'Didn't I tell you before?' she said, very quietly, very firmly. 'You keep away from that lake and you leave the past alone.'

'Why, though?' he asked. 'Did someone drown or something?'

It was Eddie who answered. 'Yes. Kit Barrington did, many years ago. He fell through the ice when he was skating.'

'How the heck do *you* know about that?' Tilly cried.

'My grandmother told me,' Eddie admitted. 'She said he haunted this place for years afterwards.'

'He haunted the lake, not the house,' Tilly corrected him, and sternly too. 'I know because I saw him there. I fell through the ice myself, and he saved my life, ten years to the day after he died.'

Stan rubbed his forehead. He should've left just now before things got strange. Before Tilly's story had him rooted to the spot.

'A *ghost* saved your life?' he asked. Standing here in

the morning sunshine it sounded a load of old baloney, yet he found himself somehow believing her.

There *was* something unusual about Frost Hollow Hall. He hadn't just imagined it. Last night in the hall the air had been icy cold. It'd felt like someone was watching him all the way down the stairs. And what about the mystery woman who sat on people's beds, waking them up in the middle of the night? And Kit Barrington himself, whose grave yesterday gave him the heebie-jeebies, and whose ice skate, he was pretty sure now, it was that he'd found packed away in that box below stairs.

It was all an eerie coincidence.

'You don't have to believe me.' Tilly pulled her shawl tightly about her. 'No one did at the time apart from Will Potter, *Mr* Potter, my husband, as he later became. But that lake is a bad business, mark my words. No one has swum in it since the day Kit died: we don't dare to. It's not safe, and certainly not just for a game.'

Stan felt his innards twist. 'But my sister's there now, swimming. I've got to stop her, haven't I?'

'You'd blinkin' well better!' Tilly agreed.

'What's the quickest way from here?'

'Follow the path, turn right. Keep going. You'll

come to a gate. And you, Mr American, had better go with him,' Tilly called out. 'Here, take this, just in case.' From the pile of horse equipment, she managed to pull out a decent length of rope.

In case of what? Stan thought, starting to panic. Though he took the rope from her: it weighed a ton.

'For flip's sake get on with it!' Tilly yelled.

Heart thundering, Stan raced up the path, willing his puny legs to go faster. At his side, Eddie hardly broke a sweat.

'Don't worry, buddy, it'll be okay,' he kept saying.

But with June it was never simple. If Stan stopped her doing the dare, she'd never forgive him. He'd forever be the annoying little brother who ruined everything. And if he didn't stop her and something awful happened, *he'd* never forgive himself.

*

When they reached the lake, it was deserted. It didn't seem so inviting now, either, despite the hot sunshine and water that looked as cool and smooth as silk. Dotted amongst the grass were statues – not grand ones like Kit's angel: these were old, weathered, yellow-patched with lichen. It might've been very smart here once, but now the whole place had a forgotten-about, neglected feel.

What Tilly told him stuck in Stan's mind: Kit Barrington drowned in this lake. The boy in whose bedroom they all slept, whose old leather ice-skating boot he'd stuffed down his pyjama top to take upstairs to June. It really didn't sit easily with him: none of it did. He didn't care about beating Clive Spencer any more. He just wanted his sister to be safe.

'She ain't here yet,' Eddie said. 'Told you it would be okay.'

But as Stan bent double to get his wind back, he noticed footprints in the dirt. They looked like a girl's gym shoes. He was pretty certain they were June's.

Straightening up, he stared out at the lake, scanning the left side first. It was as large and daunting as a sea, and perhaps as deep as one too, the water a shadowy greeny-grey. Even the strongest swimmer could be overwhelmed in a place like this.

On the far side of the lake, he thought he saw something move.

'What's that?' he asked, pointing. 'There, look, by those big trees! On the far bank!'

Eddie saw it. 'It's a girl! A blonde one!'

June had blonde hair.

First Stan felt relief, then a great wave of fear as Eddie drew a sharp breath. 'Jeepers, buddy, looks like she's in trouble!'

10

They stood no chance of reaching June from their side of the lake. Luckily, the path hugged the water's edge all the way round: at a frantic sprint, they followed it until they came to a clump of beech trees. Here, at a spot where the bank jutted out, they found June's shoes and school skirt folded neatly on the grass. On top of it, gleaming dangerously in the sunshine, was the left-footed ice skate.

There was no sign of her in the water any more.

'June!' Stan yelled, spinning around, looking everywhere. 'June!'

He felt sick that they were too late, that she'd already gone under. Scrambling down the bank, he stood shin deep in the water, gasping at the coldness of it.

'No, buddy.' Eddie dropped down beside him. 'I need you to wait on the bank.'

About sixty feet out on the lake, the water stirred. June bobbed to the surface, spluttering, coughing, doing a very weak doggy paddle.

'June!' Stan yelled in relief. 'It's going to be all right! I'm coming to get you!'

'Give me that.' Eddie gestured to the rope slung over his shoulder.

'What're you going to do?' Stan asked.

'What *you're* going to do is tie it round one of those trees, and when I say so, pull like I'm a big old fish on a line.'

'But she's my sister!' Stan argued. 'And I'm a really good swimmer!'

Eddie held out his hand for the rope. There wasn't time to discuss it. Being a soldier, Eddie would have training in survival stuff and know what he was doing. And there was the simple fact that he was far bigger and stronger than Stan.

'Hurry up, then,' Stan muttered, giving him the rope.

Eddie surged away into the deeper water. 'Miss?' he called, hands cupped to his mouth. 'I'm coming to get you, okay?'

Climbing back up on to the bank, his feet squelching in his shoes, Stan found the nearest tree and wrapped his end of the rope around it. That done, all he could do now was wait for the signal to pull.

It was scarier, somehow, watching from the bank.

Though Eddie powered through the water with a strong front crawl, June kept sinking beneath the surface. It was like she was drunk with cold. Gritting his teeth, Stan willed Eddie on. Inch by very slow inch, as he got closer to June, the rope that connected them unravelled at Stan's feet.

'Hold on, June!' he yelled encouragingly. 'Eddie'll get you out, don't worry!'

He kept shouting, repeating it like a stuck record. And it did the trick because June was now getting cross.

'Shut up! Stop fussing!' she cried as her head bobbed above the water.

Once Eddie reached her, he tied the rope around her chest, his cold fingers fumbling at the knot.

'I'm going to pull,' he told June. 'And Stan's going to pull too, got it?'

Stan nodded. Grabbing the rope, he wound it round his hands, gripping as tight as he could.

Out in the water, though, June started struggling. She was trying to undo Eddie's knot and pushing him away.

'No!' she shouted, and something else that sounded like, 'Not me!'

Each time she tried to speak her mouth filled with

water. She was weakening too, sinking, then floating. Stan was pretty sure this wasn't meant to happen, and it scared him. Eddie, who was trying to calm her down, finally lost his patience.

'Cut it out, miss, I want to help!' he cried.

'Don't save me!' June shouted.

But Eddie waved to Stan to start pulling. He dug his heels into the ground, heaving so hard he was practically on his back. A whoosh in the water. Eddie, dragging June, was coming in fast to the bank.

When they were in water shallow enough to stand, June slumped against Eddie. Her legs were too weak to hold her, so he carried her the rest of the way, before putting her down on the bank. Stan, weak himself from pulling so hard, let go of the rope and rushed over. He took off his sweater and put it round June's shoulders. She was shivering violently.

Eddie made her get to her feet. 'You need to warm up, miss. Keep moving. Get the blood flowing.'

'Thaaa ...' June tried to protest but her teeth were chattering so hard she couldn't get her words out. She still couldn't stand, either.

'Shouldn't we get help?' Stan asked worriedly. 'Or take her back to the house?'

Eddie, shaking the water off himself, nodded

towards the path. 'Looks like the house is coming to us.'

Sure enough, a crowd of people were hurrying towards them along the path: the other GIs, Miss Potter, Miss Barrington, Gladys the horse, Mr Potter, and with him, hanging on to his arm, Tilly. Even the sausage dogs, little Lobelia included, were bounding over the grass.

On reaching them, everyone crowded round. June was wrapped in blankets and given brandy from Miss Potter's flask. The relief that his sister was safe made Stan's limbs turn to jelly. He was exhausted. But as Mr Potter and Eddie tried to get her up on to Gladys to take her back to the house, she struggled to speak again, her voice thick and slurred with cold.

'No!' she cried. 'It's not just me! Please! You have to listen!'

Stan was bewildered. 'What's she trying to tell us? What's happened?'

It was Tilly who finally understood, the colour draining from her face. 'Oh heck, someone's still in the water.'

There couldn't be; the surface of the lake was empty. Unless the person was under the water . . .

Stan's first thought was Clive. He'd said he was

coming here, hadn't he? He must've got to the lake first, and been already swimming when June arrived.

So why then was Clive on the bank with the others, looking shaken up but completely dry and warm?

Stan's heart stopped.

The one person he couldn't see was Maggie.

*

Blocking out shouts of 'Stay back!', 'Don't be stupid!', 'Someone stop him!', he half crawled, half scrambled into the lake. Behind him, Stan was aware of other people throwing themselves into the water. He was fastest, though. The cold made him catch his breath, but he kept kicking until he was at least as far out as June had been.

Beneath him the water was black. He couldn't see anything down there: it was like staring into a witch's cauldron. He was aware of the cold seeping through his shirt. His knees in their short trousers had already gone numb. Out of the corner of his eye he saw Eddie inching towards him, demanding he go back to the bank and leave it to the adults.

Stan didn't listen. Pinching his nose, he took a few short, sharp breaths. Kicking up with his feet, he dived under with his eyes wide open, going down and down into darkness. It wasn't pitch-black, but a swirling, soupy brown that smelled of mud and was so cold it felt like someone was squeezing his brain in a vice. He despaired at finding Maggie in this.

Instinct took over. He swam in gentle strokes that didn't use too much energy. As the seconds ticked by, his lungs began to fold up. He imagined them like those funny paper shapes June made to tell her friends who they were going to marry. That was how his brain was working: it was slowing down, relaxing.

He grew calmer with it. And instead of seeing nothing but darkness, the water grew lighter, so light, in fact, it was almost like gloomy daylight, and queer as anything.

Queerest of all was seeing Maggie coming towards him.

She couldn't swim – none of them had taught her yet. Yet here she was, gliding through the water like a fish, even though she still wore her school pinafore and black lace-up shoes.

Stan didn't know what to do. What it meant.

Had he got to her in time? Were they both dead? In Tilly's story Kit Barrington's ghost saved her life; was Maggie about to save his?

Well, he didn't want that to be their story. There were enough ghosts here at Frost Hollow Hall, and he didn't want to join them.

Grabbing Maggie's hand, he started paddling upwards. She tried to let go. Shaking her head and clawing at his arm, she was pointing back down to the lake bed, where he could see a blade, an ice skate – the right-footed one, it must be – glinting in the mud. He kept swimming. She was fighting, trying to drag him back to the skate. Oh, how he wished he'd left that wretched thing in the cupboard.

Above them, the water churned with people reaching down to grab them. Someone seized Stan's shirt and pulled. They both shot up, Maggie and him, out of the water, into the daylight. On the bank, Stan lay back, exhausted. All he could think was how warm the grass felt beneath him.

Maggie, though, was sick all over Mr Potter's shoes.

11

It took days to warm up again, longer still to get the smell of lake out of their hair and the mud from under their fingernails. As Tilly's cottage was cosier, she offered to look after Stan and his sisters until they'd recovered. All three siblings shared a small back bedroom, which was exactly how Stan had wanted things from the start. It meant squeezing into one bed, but listening to Maggie's snoring, or waking up with June's feet in his face, was a small price to pay.

On that very first night, when they were still shivery and weak and tucked up in bed, he and June finally cleared the air.

'You shouldn't have let Maggot come with you. You knew she couldn't swim,' Stan said. He didn't want to make June feel guilty, but he was trying to be more direct because that was how she often spoke to him.

'I know.' June hung her head. 'It was stupid of me. All I was thinking about was finding that bloomin' ice skate.'

'The game was a crummy idea anyway,' Stan said. 'It was just an excuse for Clive Spencer to show off.'

'It was my idea too,' June pointed out.

'And I won the first dare,' Maggie added sleepily.

June sighed. She smoothed out the bedclothes in a way that meant she had something important to say. 'You know who the winner was in the end, though, don't you?'

Stan didn't.

'You.' She sounded almost sheepish. 'You did the most daring thing out of all of us – and for the best reasons too.'

'But I didn't think, either,' he insisted, feeling himself go red. 'I just wanted Maggot to be safe and you to stop being angry.'

June went quiet. Between them, Maggie started to snore.

'It's better to be careful than be stupid,' June said quietly. 'You were right to worry about Mum that night, when she couldn't stop coughing. You didn't know a bomb was going to drop on us – you were just caring for Mum, that was all. You're a very decent brother – the best, in fact. I'm sorry I've been such a cow.'

Stan blinked. His sister had never apologised for anything. Though she didn't mention their brother Donnie by name, he knew what she was trying to say.

He couldn't remember hearing her talk in such a thoughtful way. He liked it – just as much, if not more than the bold brave June who didn't back down from anything.

He felt the need to explain himself too. 'I know I get scared and I'm not tough like you, but after today, well, maybe scared people *can* be brave sometimes, if they have to be, I mean.'

'Too right they can,' June agreed.

*

The next day Eddie came to say goodbye. Now the truck had been fixed, the Americans were on their way to the south coast, though no one was supposed to know that. Waving away Tilly's offer of tea and a currant bun, Eddie said he'd just wanted to check the children were recovering. It was true – but only partly. And Tilly sensed it.

'I'd like a word with you myself,' she said, and

made him take a seat by the fire.

Poor Eddie couldn't keep still. It was bizarre to see the same soldier who'd dived into a lake and rescued his sister, now struggling to be brave. Stan and his sisters crammed themselves into the nearest armchair, desperate to hear what this was all about.

'So, young man, what I want to know is how your grandmother knew about Kit Barrington,' Tilly said.

Eddie held up his hands. 'You got me, ma'am. I'd better start from the beginning. It wasn't an accident, I'm afraid I deliberately crashed the truck outside Frost Hollow Hall.'

'Wowsers!' Stan whistled. So Lalit *was* right, after all – he couldn't wait to tell him.

Tilly glared at Eddie. 'Why the heck would anyone drive a truck into a ditch on purpose? Are you sure you're right in the head, young man?'

She didn't mince her words, and Stan almost laughed. But he saw the beads of sweat on Eddie's brow. The poor chap really was nervous.

'Promise me you won't tell anyone,' he pleaded.

They all nodded.

'Scout's honour,' Stan added, saluting.

'I had to come here, to see you, Tilly. But they wouldn't have allowed it if I'd asked,' Eddie explained.

'As we were heading south on an exercise, and I knew this place wasn't far away, well, I said I'd do the driving and—'

Eddie stopped to reach down into his kitbag. He pulled out a package wrapped in brown paper, then took a very deep breath. 'This is why I came to Frost Hollow Hall.'

What he gave Tilly looked the size and shape of a pot of jam. It was kind of him, Stan supposed. Yet he couldn't see why Eddie would fake an accident just to bring jam when Tilly probably had loads of it in her larder already.

'Oh,' said Tilly, who seemed to be thinking the same. 'Ta very much.'

As she started to unwrap it, Eddie grew jumpier than ever. It was making Stan feel edgy now too.

'I'd better explain,' Eddie blurted out. 'My name is Edward Johnson. My grandmother, on my mother's side, is called Eliza.'

Tilly's hands went still.

'Who's Eliza?' June hissed in Stan's ear, but he didn't know, either.

Eddie hurried on. 'My grandmother came to America in the spring of 1881, so she tells me. She arrived in New York with her father – he was your father too, wasn't he, Tilly?'

Stan's mouth fell open. Crikey, Eliza must be the sister Tilly hadn't spoken to in over sixty years. Even for him, it was a shock.

'My mother gave me Kit Barrington's middle name – Edward.' Eddie kept talking, getting into his stride. 'She never forgot what my grandmother told her about him rescuing you from the lake. I grew up hearing that story, time and time again. And so you see, Tilly, you're my family too – my great-aunt – and I sure as heck wanted to meet you.'

As Eddie told her this, Tilly's face was like a hillside on a sunny day when clouds are racing overhead: the colour of it, the mood, kept changing. Stan found it rather hard to watch.

'My sister – your grandmother,' Tilly said shakily, 'left our village all those years ago without a thought for anyone but herself. She lured my father away from me, don't you see? In bettering her own life, she broke my mother's heart into little pieces, and trampled all over mine.'

There wasn't much anyone could say to that, though June tried. 'Being cross with someone doesn't feel very nice, not forever.'

But Stan could see it from Tilly's side too. Sixty years was a very long time not to speak to someone. She probably wouldn't even recognise Eliza any more, let alone know what to say to her.

In her lap still was the jar-shaped gift, which she half-heartedly began picking at again.

'Eliza wanted it to come back to you, where it belonged,' Eddie said rather cryptically.

With the wrappings finally off, Tilly held up a brass pot with an inscription on the side. It wasn't like any jar of jam Stan had ever seen.

'What is it, Tilly?' Maggie asked, eyes like saucers. 'Is it treasure?'

As she turned the pot over in her hands, there was a moment – a lighting up – when Tilly seemed to realise what it was.

'No, lovey,' she replied, in a voice that shook. 'It's worth more to me than treasure.'

Very slowly, very carefully, she placed it between them on the table. The pot was small, plain, with a screw-on lid. Stan had once seen something similar when his gran died. Mum kept it under her bed – *had* kept it under the bed. He recognised it as a pot that contained a dead person's ashes.

'Will!' Tilly was now on her feet, wiping her hands in her skirt and calling to Mr Potter in the kitchen. 'Get in here, can you?'

He appeared in the doorway. 'What's the matter, dear?'

Tilly pointed to the jar. 'My sister sent him back to me, Will. All these years Eliza had Pa all to herself. Now, at last, she's sent him home again.'

There were lots of tears – happy ones, mostly. When Eddie left, he scribbled down Eliza's address and gave it to Tilly.

'I'm glad to have met my English family, ma'am,' he said, touching his cap. 'Your sister's a strong woman.'

Tilly laughed. 'Yes, she is that.' Then she took Eddie's hand. 'And you, my great-nephew, are a credit to Kit's name.'

Afterwards, when Mr Potter mentioned he had a writing pad upstairs and did she want it, Tilly said she'd think about it, which after sixty years of silence was probably a start.

*

A week or so later, Stan, June and Maggie were considered well enough to rejoin the others at the hall. Before they left, Tilly took Stan to one side.

'You didn't see anyone under the water that day, did you?' she asked, searching his face. 'A boy, I mean, in a white shirt?'

Understanding what she was getting at, Stan shook his head. 'There weren't any ghosts down there, I promise.'

'Thank goodness.' Tilly relaxed a little.

'I saw the ice skate, though. Right down at the bottom it was, sunk into the mud.'

'You didn't touch it, did you?' Tilly asked.

'No, I left it where it was.'

Tilly sighed. Patted his arm. 'You're a good lad, Stan. I just want Kit Barrington to rest in peace, that's all.'

'Something odd *did* happen, mind you,' Stan admitted. 'It was almost light down there, far more than you'd expect water at that depth to be. And Maggie was swimming, even though she doesn't know how to, and I felt really calm. I can't describe it, but it was pretty strange.'

Tilly smiled. 'You don't have to, son. I know exactly what you mean.'

*

There weren't any ghosts inside Frost Hollow Hall, either. The woman who'd been visiting sad, homesick children in the night wasn't a mysterious, restless spirit, but Miss Barrington herself. Little Sadie told them the news almost as soon as they got back.

'How do you know it was her?' June was amazed. 'Did she tell you?'

'Sort of,' the girl replied. 'Last time she came, I put my torch on.'

'Good work!' Stan said.

'She's proper nice, she really is,' Sadie gushed. 'We shouldn't have been scared of her, she's only trying to be kind.'

Stan was puzzled. 'But why come in the middle of the night? It's all a bit secretive, isn't it?'

'She's awful shy, that's what she is,' Sadie said. 'Says sausage dogs are easier than people.'

'I don't think Lobelia's that easy,' Maggie piped up.

'Miss Barrington came to me when I was having a bad dream one night,' June confided. 'What about you, Sadie? Were you having nightmares?'

'I was crying.' Sadie nodded. 'Every night I got upset she'd come and hold my hand.'

'But I thought she didn't want us here,' Stan said, still confused. 'We were told to keep away from the East Wing, and from her. The army made her take us in, remember.'

'Maybe she didn't realise she liked children until she met some,' June suggested, then glanced sideways at

Stan. 'None of us asked for this situation, did we? But sometimes people can surprise you.'

They also discovered from Tilly that Miss Barrington and Miss Potter lived together in the East Wing with the dogs that Miss Barrington often called her 'fur family'.

'Who'd have thought it, eh? The baronet's daughter and my girl from the village,' Tilly said, cackling with laughter. 'A Barrington and a Higgins, together at last!'

Clive Spencer, meanwhile, kept a respectful distance from Stan and his sisters. He probably never found out about Stan's double dealing, but he accepted with surprisingly good grace that the girls' team had won the game of dare. When the postman arrived one day with letters from home, he waited in line for his, just as excited as everyone else. It seemed that even show-offs got homesick.

The letter from Mum was short, but very cheering. Her leg was coming out of plaster next week, and once that was done she'd catch the bus down to visit them.

'I've missed you all so much,' June read out. 'The house can be replaced, never mind that, but you lot can't be. Wherever we live next, as long as we're together, it'll be our home. Perhaps we can get ourselves a pet too.'

'Oh! Can we have a dog?' Maggie pleaded.

June looked at Stan, who shrugged. 'I don't mind. I quite like them these days.'

Returning to the letter, June grinned at something scribbled at the bottom. 'Oh ace! She's promising to take us for fish and chips when she comes!'

Maggie whooped. Stan licked his lips. After weeks of rubbery porridge and bone soup, the thought of haddock, chips and the biggest pickled onion in the jar made his mouth well and truly water. He'd waited long enough.

OLIVE'S ARMY

1

It was typical of my sister Sukie to shock the living daylights out of us.

'By the way,' she said one Sunday afternoon as she was trimming my little brother's hair. 'I'm getting married.'

Cliff twisted round so fast he was lucky not to lose an ear. Thankfully, I was at a safe distance from the haircutting scissors, and lowered the book I'd been reading. '*Married?* What, to Ephraim?'

Sukie laughed. 'Oh, Olive! Of course to *Ephraim*, you great 'nana!' like I was the stupid one, when only yesterday she'd claimed marriage was for idiots.

Yet I'd heard her saying it – it was impossible not to, living as we did, with Ephraim in his lighthouse. Sound had a way of travelling between each floor. She and Ephraim had been arguing about whether Hitler *could* still invade Britain, like people had been fearing these past couple of years.

'It won't happen now,' Ephraim assured her. 'He's too busy fighting on the Eastern Front.'

'Huh!' Sukie replied. 'I'd put nothing past *him*. Well, he can try it. I'll be ready.'

'You'd fight, would you?'

''Course I would!'

'You'd kill another human being with your bare hands? Even a German?' Ephraim was getting angry, which was unusual for him.

'Not my bare hands, no!' Sukie bit back. 'I'd use a garden fork! Or a kitchen one if I had to!'

Things escalated. There'd been door-slamming, and furious feet stomping down the stairs. They made it up again by teatime, mind you. By then half the village knew they'd had a barney, which was how life was in Budmouth Point.

When we'd come here almost a year and a half ago as London evacuees, it'd been tough. The locals were a suspicious bunch, not to mention Esther Jenkins as we knew her then, who I was convinced had accompanied us from London just to make life hell. All I'd wanted was to go home.

Funny how things turn out.

Nowadays, Budmouth Point felt as much our home as London. Esther Wirth, as was her proper name, was my dearest pal. The locals, who'd seemed so unwelcoming, were in fact some of the kindest, bravest people I'd ever met once you got to know them.

While Cliff and I lived with Ephraim at the lighthouse, Sukie and Esther each had a room above the post office, which was owned by the postmistress, Queenie. The living quarters there were huge and rambling, and so old that the upstairs part didn't have electricity. It was this I was thinking of now, because once people got married, they tended to live together.

'Are you moving into the lighthouse?' I asked my sister. If there was one thing I missed about London, it was us being together under the same roof.

'Possibly,' she replied.

'It'd be the wasp's ankles if you did,' I said eagerly.

Sukie hesitated. 'Ephraim and I haven't talked about where we'll live yet.'

'Oh.' I suspected there was something she wasn't telling us.

Cliff, though, leapt to his feet. 'If you marry Ephraim, he'll be family, won't he? And Pixie'll be my sister in-law!' Pixie being Ephraim's terrier, though she was just as much Cliff's these days.

'Sit down! You've only got half a haircut!' Sukie wailed.

'And only half a story,' I reminded her. 'So you'd better tell us everything.'

Sukie put down the scissors.

'Ephraim doesn't know about us getting married yet,' she confessed.

I stared at her. 'You mean he hasn't *asked* you?'

'No, Olive.' Sukie squared her shoulders, lifted her chin. '*I* haven't asked *him*.'

*

Once we'd sworn Cliff to secrecy on pain of death, and Sukie had evened up his fringe, we let him go. Sweeping up Cliff's hair trimmings from the floor, Sukie hummed jive tunes and kept saying how she couldn't wait to see Ephraim's face when she popped the question.

I should've felt more excited than I did, but couldn't shake off the argument I'd overheard yesterday. Though the threat wasn't as severe now, a German invasion *could* still happen. Hitler had dug his heels in in France, and people kept saying Britain was next on the list.

Would we really have to fight the enemy ourselves, with garden forks? Would Ephraim refuse to defend his home? Would he not fight for Sukie, for Pixie and the lighthouse?

The thought troubled me. The Nazis had killed my dad. They'd shot Esther's mum and taken away her brother. I'd seen the faces of Jews who'd fled Europe, only to turn up on Budmouth beach, still stunned with fear. If there was a very real chance of Hitler's army coming here, then I couldn't imagine for a moment standing back and letting it happen.

We got snippets and updates from Queenie, who knew far more about the war than was normal for a postmistress. What she told us only troubled me more; I almost wished she'd keep it to herself. If the Germans invaded through Devon and Cornwall, our army would fight them along a border called the Taunton Stop Line, where pillboxes and fences had been put up and ditches dug as defences. Basically, they'd get no further than Somerset. Which was all very well if you lived there, or beyond. Here to the south, in Devon, we'd be stuck with the invaders.

This past year we'd been on alert. Razor wire ran all along the clifftops. A pillbox had been built on the high path between Budmouth Point and Tythe Cove: every day someone from the Home Guard trudged up there with his sandwiches and tea flask to keep watch.

At night sometimes, when a ship went by, I'd wake up in a panic: was this it? Were the Nazis here? Then I'd hear Ephraim talking on the radio – cool, calm – and I'd turn over and go back to sleep.

Yet my own annoying doubt-voice was now whispering in my brain. Would Ephraim really not kill a Nazi to protect those he loved? Once, when a German pilot crashed near the village, I'd stood up for him, arguing that he was a person just like us. Was this any different?

I didn't know. But it was absolutely typical of Sukie to want to marry someone as complicated as she was.

*

'Ephraim might not even say yes,' Esther pointed out, as we strolled home from school the next day.

Arm in arm, we huddled together against the bracing wind that blew in Budmouth all year round, even on a hot summer's day like this one. We'd just had a whole afternoon of algebra and equations, so it was a relief to be thinking about something else.

'Don't tell her I told you,' I warned.

Esther mimed zipping her mouth shut, which wasn't something that came naturally to her. I trusted her with a big secret like this, though.

'I think it's really romantic. A proper love story,' Esther said.

'I just hope he's brave enough if the Nazis come,' I replied.

'Why?' Esther teased. 'What would you do? Whack 'em over the head with a book?'

'I'd like to think I'd fight,' I said.

Esther turned to me, serious now, the wind whipping her hair across her face. 'Olive, when something *that* terrible happens, no one knows how brave they'll be.'

I sighed miserably: she was right. Esther knew all too well what happened when the Nazis invaded your country. It was why she'd come to England with the Kindertransport in the first place. And why her dad, in trying to be with her, had become a prisoner in an internment camp on the North Devon coast.

'I'm sorry,' I said, leaning my head against her shoulder. 'I didn't mean to make you think of bad things.'

'So let's think of happy things instead,' Esther suggested. 'Like weddings.'

'Do brides wear white at Jewish weddings?' I asked.

'If they want to. It's all pretty similar really, except we have a rabbi not a vicar.'

'And it happens in a synagogue not a church?'

'Maybe. Or outside, under a chupah. It's a canopy-type thing.'

'Does the dad give the bride away?'

'Sometimes. Or the mother.'

I nodded. 'I like the sound of that.'

2

Of course, Ephraim *did* say yes. It happened one night during supper and, though I'd been expecting it, it still took me by surprise. Sukie had come over to eat with us, bringing a big jam tart for afters.

'Fetch the pudding, will you, Olive?' she asked as she cleared the supper plates.

She'd left it on the side, covered with a cloth. When I whipped it off, there it was – 'Will You Marry Me?' spelled out in pastry on the top. It gave me such a start I very nearly dropped it, which might've pleased Pixie, who was watching greedily, but would've ruined the surprise for Ephraim.

For the rest of the evening there was a lot of kissing and hugging. Ephraim, who'd apparently once said he'd never get married, looked the happiest man alive. So did Cliff, who ate most of the tart when no one was watching.

As for me, it was the moment I stopped listening

to the doubts. Ephraim and Sukie were made for each other, any fool could see that. They were very dear to me, both of them, and to watch them together, so happy, made me warm-inside happy too. No Nazi invaders were going to ruin it.

*

Once Sukie and Ephraim got the licence and had their banns read out in church, the date was set for three weeks' time. As always happened when there was something to organise, we gathered at Queenie's kitchen table to drink horribly weak tea.

'Would you believe the last time someone got married in Budmouth church was 1937?' Mrs Henderson told us. She was small, round, tweed-clad and smelled slightly of goats, and since our time in Budmouth had become like a favourite aunt to Cliff and me.

'Will it be in the church?' asked Queenie. 'Only, you know they won't ring the bells, don't you?'

It was one of those wartime rules which meant Sunday mornings were very quiet these days. The bells would only be rung to warn us if the Germans were invading. And it wouldn't be a lovely tuneful peal, but terrible, non-stop ringing.

Thankfully, Esther moved on to more cheery matters. 'Can I do your hair? Oh let me, Sukie!'

'I'll make the cake. You can do a lovely sponge with goat butter,' Mrs Henderson told us. Cliff, who'd come along because he was bored, pulled a sick face, though I knew as well as he did he'd eat any sort of cake.

'What about the dress?' Queenie asked. 'Even if we all club together, we won't have enough coupons for anything decent.'

Sukie had already thought of that, and sketched out what she wanted on the back of an envelope. A very chic-looking dress that was definitely going to be the cat's pyjamas.

'And something similar for Olive and Esther as my bridesmaids,' she said, looking at me. 'That's if you both fancy it?'

Which we did. Very, very much.

*

The next couple of weeks passed in a whirl. Then finally, two days before the wedding, Mum arrived from London. We went to meet her off the four o'clock train – *we* being Sukie, Esther and me, and Cliff, who insisted Pixie needed a walk. The station was surprisingly busy so we had to stand on tiptoe to find Mum in the crowds. Everywhere you looked were kitbags and suitcases, trilby hats and army caps. Pixie thought it all good fun and kept trying to jump up at everyone who went by.

'Keep that dog under control,' Sukie warned us. But when Pixie lunged at a passing soldier, she was all smiles. 'I'm so sorry, she's got no manners.'

'No problem, ma'am,' the man replied.

Hearing his accent, Esther and I clutched each other in delight: *'An American!'*

The only place I'd ever come across American voices was at the movies. To hear one right in front of us made Esther and me go a bit giggly.

'Oh stop it, you two!' Sukie laughed.

The soldier moved on. The crowd cleared a little, and there, coming towards us, was Mum.

I'd not seen her since Christmas, when she'd still been recovering from Dad's death and was so thin her clothes hung off her like a scarecrow's. Today she was wearing a yellow summer frock that fitted perfectly. And she was smiling – a huge, beaming lighthouse of a smile. I was overjoyed to see her looking so well.

'Congratulations, love.' Mum wrapped Sukie into the tightest hug, only breaking away to give Cliff and me a lipsticky kiss, and Esther an affectionate tweak on her cheek. 'A wedding in the family, eh? Isn't it exciting?'

Whilst we'd been greeting Mum, the station had got even busier. There were American soldiers everywhere now, streaming off another train in a sea of khaki uniforms and suntanned faces. They were so tall, so handsome, so *healthy*. It was like being in the front row at the pictures, only these were real soldiers, not actors, and they were here, right before our eyes.

'They can't all be here for your wedding, Sukie,' Cliff remarked. 'Can they?'

'Of course not, you daftie.' Sukie laughed.

They were here for some reason, though, and it threw a shadow over things, rather. A train full of GIs didn't arrive at Budmouth Point every day of the week. I just hoped they weren't expecting trouble.

*

By Friday afternoon, everything was ready. Sukie, amazing as ever, had turned a pair of Mrs Henderson's brocade curtains into her wedding frock and a bridesmaid's outfit each for Esther and me. The cake, done with goat butter, turned out pretty well too, and by the time we'd decorated the church pews with seashells from the beach, things didn't look too shoddy at all.

'It's perfect,' Sukie declared, as we drank our final cup of tea at Queenie's kitchen table that evening. 'I can't thank you enough for all you've done.'

It was one of those special moments. I felt warm and light and happy. Even the fact that Dad wasn't here didn't spoil things because we still had each other, and tomorrow was going to be brilliant.

Then Esther chipped in with, 'What's Cliff done, exactly? Apart from eating all the biscuits.'

At the end of the table, my brother was trying – and failing – to get Pixie to lie down and roll over. Hearing his name, he looked up. 'What've I done?'

'Nothing towards the wedding, apparently,' I told him. 'We should get you to read at the service or show people to their seats in church.'

'I have done something, *actually*,' he said, glaring at Esther.

She smirked. 'Like what?'

He folded his arms, looking all smug. 'It's a secret. You'll have to wait till tomorrow, won't you?'

3

Later that evening, I called Cliff for supper.

'Wash your hands!' I shouted. 'Food's ready!'

Cliff didn't reply. He hadn't appeared by the time I'd laid the table and cut bread. After searching indoors, I realised he was still down on the beach with Pixie.

'Supper time!' I yelled, from the top of the lighthouse ladder.

The view from up here was terrific, once you'd got used to being so high. You could see almost all of Budmouth Point village in one swoop, which was how I came to spot the tents – twenty of them at least, pitched just beyond the beach in one of Mrs Henderson's fields. Milling about between them, carrying boxes and calling to each other, were the American soldiers.

I couldn't wait to tell Esther. Both of us were fascinated by the GIs. Apparently, they carried sweets in their pockets for us local kids. They had money to spend too, and people said they'd pay anything for a decent cup of coffee, which was what they missed most about home. The fact they were camping at Mrs Henderson's meant she might let us actually meet a few, or at the very least spy on them from her living-room window.

Meanwhile, Cliff still hadn't heard me. In the end I had to go down to the beach, and even then he didn't notice until I was standing right in front of him.

'Crikey, Olive!' He clutched his chest. 'Talk about giving a lad a heart attack!'

'Didn't you hear me calling?' I was a bit tetchy, to be honest. All I wanted was to eat my supper and then curl up with a book, not be chasing round after my little brother.

Yet Cliff looked as if he'd just won a hundred pounds.

'I've finally got her to do the trick!' He grinned. 'In time for tomorrow!'

He meant Pixie, who was sitting expectantly at his feet. So this was what he'd been up to the past few days – teaching her something special for the wedding. It was such a sweet idea and so typically Cliff, I couldn't help smiling.

'Go on, then,' I said, hugging my cardigan against

me, because the wind off the sea was fierce. 'Let's see her do it.'

From his pocket, Cliff pulled out a stale crust of bread. Pixie licked her lips.

'Now stay.' Cliff started walking backwards, still holding the bread out so she could see it.

He kept going until he was dangerously near the water's edge. I wondered what he was doing, but thought it best to keep my gob shut. Especially as Pixie seemed to know exactly what was going on. She sat very still, every muscle quivering.

'Bring 'em here!' Cliff called.

And just like that, she was up, not with her usual mad scrabbling but picking her way daintily across the shingle. She managed it for all of five or six yards, before something in the sea behind Cliff caught her eye.

The shingle went flying. In a whirl of white fur, yapping wildly, Pixie charged down the beach.

'Oi!' I shouted. 'Come back here!'

She ran straight past Cliff and into the sea until she was chest deep in the water. I sprinted after her. Cliff spun round, confused.

'What's she doing?' he cried. 'What's she found?'

She was about ten yards out, at the spot where the waves foamed just before the sea got deeper. Beside her something was floating in the water. Something big. Person-sized.

'Oh no.' I pulled at Cliff's arm, as it hit me what it was. You heard stories sometimes of bodies turning up if an enemy plane got shot down and the pilot had ejected. This one looked as if he had drowned. I didn't want to go any closer. 'Come away. We'll fetch Ephraim. He'll know what to do.'

But blasted Pixie wouldn't budge. She kept barking. And barking.

'She's trying to tell us something,' Cliff said. 'She wants us to pull it in.'

The body lay face down in the surf. Though I was trying not to, I could see it was a man in a dark coat, with a bag strapped across his back. He was tall, and waterlogged. Between us, I didn't think we stood a chance of getting him out of the water.

But Pixie was right. We couldn't just leave him there. If the sea carried him too far up the beach, he'd end up caught in the razor wire and that would be horrid too. I pushed up my sleeves.

'All right,' I said. 'We'll give it a try.'

Before we could, a huge wave broke over Pixie's head. For one terrifying moment we couldn't see her. The sea rushed towards us, and suddenly we were knee deep in churning, foaming water. Then Pixie bobbed up again, paddling to stay afloat.

'Grab her!' Cliff yelled.

I was able to get my arms around her and pull her up on to my hip. The man's body went spinning past us up the beach. As quick as the wave came in, it pulled away again, leaving the body high and dry.

Cliff reached it first.

'Don't look. It might be horrible,' I warned as I struggled up the beach after him. But he was already standing over the person, who seemed to have paperwork spilling soggily from his pocket.

Cliff poked the papers with his toe. 'Do those say what I *think* they do?'

Warily, I crouched down, still keeping a tight hold of Pixie. The writing was typed. But the name was the same on each sheet, and even the envelopes: 'Ephraim Pengilly'.

Clear as day. There for anyone to see.

'I don't like it, Olive,' Cliff said.

I didn't, either. In fact, I felt like I'd been slapped in the face.

'Why would a dead man be carrying letters for Ephraim?' Cliff asked.

'I don't know.' I glanced back along the beach at the

lighthouse, standing tall in the thickening dusk, and could hear that little doubt-voice again.

Ephraim, who had secrets of his own.

I told myself to stop it. Just because there was a war on, it didn't make it all right to question everyone over everything. Ephraim was decent through and through, and always had been. There was probably some quite ordinary explanation for all this.

'Here, hold the dog a sec.' I handed Pixie to Cliff. 'I'm going to check his pockets.'

'Shouldn't we get a grown-up to do that?' Cliff sounded nervous.

'I'll be quick,' I assured him.

Kneeling down properly, I prodded the lump of paper. Everything was so wet, it was impossible to peel the letters and envelopes apart.

'What do they say?' Cliff demanded.

'I don't know. Everything's in German.'

'But Ephraim doesn't know any Germans,' Cliff insisted.

'Not that he's told us about,' I said grimly.

That wasn't the worst of it. In between the letters was a card – like an identity card, I supposed, with a name and address on it – the sort of thing we all had to carry these days. I didn't have a torch, but in the gathering dark, it looked valid enough. There was an official stamp with a date and the word 'Hamburg' on it. Beneath were what seemed to be personal details. It was the name – an *English* name – that jumped off the page.

Name: Ephraim Pengilly
Adresse: Elberstrasse 10, Dresden.
Alter: 23
Beruf: Kommunikationsnetz

I didn't understand. How could there be two men with the same unusual name? If this stranger, lying face down on Budmouth beach, *was* Ephraim Pengilly, then who was the person at the lighthouse with whom we were about to eat our supper?

4

Normally I'd have run to *our* Ephraim for help, but Queenie was our next best option. Esther was the only one downstairs when we arrived.

'What on earth's eating you?' she said, seeing our shocked faces.

I took a long breath. 'There's a drowned German man on the beach, and the papers he's carrying say he's called Ephraim Pengilly.'

It sounded even more ridiculous saying it out loud. Esther made me repeat it twice over before she grasped what I was trying to tell her.

'Wait there,' she said then went into the hallway and bellowed up the stairs. 'Queenie! Sukie! Mrs Bradshaw! You'd better get down here!'

*

Sukie didn't believe a word of it.

'What a load of baloney! Someone's using his name!' she insisted. And still in her hair curlers and old slacks, she ran straight out of the door for the lighthouse.

'The dead man could well be a spy,' Queenie said. 'I bet Hitler's behind this.'

Just the mention of his name made Esther flinch. 'He's the one we can't trust,' she said bitterly.

No one considered for a second that Ephraim himself might be involved. Why would they? He was everyone's very dear friend. But we still had the problem of a dead German on the beach, and Sukie running about the streets.

'I'd better let the proper people know,' Queenie said, sounding thoroughly fed up. A dead body meant telling Mr Spratt the coastguard, and the fact the man was German meant the army would also have to be alerted.

As Queenie went to raise the alarm, and Esther made a pot of tea, I noticed how quiet Mum was. I'd assumed it was because she was reassuring Cliff, who'd told everyone he'd never seen a dead person before, then burst into tears. But I sensed something else was bothering her.

'Mum?' I said. 'You've got your thoughtful look on.'

'Have I?' She shook herself out of it. 'Sorry, love. I was miles away.'

'Thinking about Dad?' I asked, because up until this evening, he'd been on my mind a lot too.

'No, Ephraim, actually.' Shifting her arm from around Cliff's shoulders, she sat up straight. 'How much do we know about him, really?'

'Oh come on, Mum!' Cliff groaned. 'We live with him. We know him as well as anyone. He's the bee's—'

'Pyjamas,' I cut in.

Esther, who'd been clanking teacups in the background, agreed. 'Honestly, Mrs Bradshaw, he's a diamond,' she insisted. 'He's done so much to help people. My papa wouldn't be here in England if it wasn't for Sukie and Ephraim.'

'Nor would plenty of others,' I added.

'Fair enough. Point taken.' Though I could tell she wasn't entirely convinced.

And it bothered me. If Mum didn't trust Ephraim, what did *that* mean? But who was I to question her? I'd had my own doubts about him too and it made me feel mixed up and horribly guilty. This was meant to be a happy time, but everything had turned on its head.

Queenie, meanwhile, returned all too quickly from making telephone calls.

'Typical!' she cried, taking off her glasses and giving them a furious polish in her sweater hem. 'Mr Spratt can't come until the morning. I've never known such a useless coastguard!'

Esther, in disgust, muttered a foreign-sounding word. None of us liked Mr Spratt, and with good reason. He was a small-minded, self-important bigot.

When, last spring, a boatload of desperate Jewish refugees had landed here from Occupied France, he'd claimed it was all Ephraim's doing and that he was breaking the law. Because he had no proof – the boat wasn't recorded in the lighthouse logbook – he'd had Queenie arrested instead. Of course, it *was* Ephraim's doing: getting that boat in safely was *all* of our doing. But rather than a mission to help frightened people, Mr Spratt saw it only as a criminal act. He'd been dying for a chance to get one over on Ephraim ever since. This situation, I could see now, would be the perfect chance.

'Do we really want him poking around?' I asked.

'We can't just leave the body on the beach, out in the open,' Queenie replied, raising her eyebrows at Cliff. 'It's rather distressing for people.'

'It wasn't that bad,' Cliff lied.

Mum stood up. Swapping her dressing gown for her overcoat, she motioned for Queenie to do the same.

Even though it wasn't her house, it was obvious who was now in charge.

'Let's fetch him in,' Mum announced. It occurred to me this probably wasn't the first time she'd come across a dead body.

'Don't expect me to help carry him,' Esther warned. 'I'm not touching a Nazi.'

I wasn't sure I wanted to, either.

*

Down on the beach, darkness had almost fallen. The wind was still strong, the surf pounding. It was hard to imagine this was a summer's night, when it felt almost as tense and grim as the time last year we'd been down here in the dark, pulling people from the sea.

'Why don't you wait up by the road?' I whispered to Cliff, who seemed to be hanging back.

'I'm not a baby,' he replied huffily.

The truth was none of us wanted to pick up the body. The man lay where we'd left him, his coat spread out like a cape. He looked thick-set, as if he'd be a fair old weight to carry, and at a guess about thirty years old. His hair, already starting to dry, was blond and recently clipped at the neck: you could just about see the white line above his suntan. I wondered if he feared, when he got that haircut, that very soon afterwards he'd be dead.

The more I looked at the body, the more ridiculous it all seemed. If this man was a German spy claiming to be an English lighthouse keeper, then he'd really not done his research. He didn't *look* remotely like the real Ephraim.

We'd just agreed who was going to grab which arm or leg, when another torch beam came swinging towards us across the beach. I hoped it might be Sukie, or Ephraim himself, but it was Mrs Henderson. With her, we quickly saw, was a group of American soldiers. The one who seemed to be in charge introduced himself as Colonel Bagatelli.

'Ladies,' he announced, 'if you could all stand back. We've got this.'

There was a split second where I thought Queenie and Mum weren't going to move. But I think even they could see the benefits of someone else carrying a sopping-wet corpse up the main street.

5

Back at the post office, it was agreed the body should stay outside overnight. The coolest, safest spot was on the path that ran through Queenie's vegetable patch. As the man's pockets were emptied, the soldiers became especially interested in one particular piece of paper, crowding together to pore over it and talk in voices so annoyingly hushed we couldn't hear what they were saying. Soon everything – the letters with Ephraim's name on, the identity card – was in Colonel Bagatelli's hands.

'Do NOT touch anything else!' Colonel Bagatelli addressed Mum and Queenie as if they were halfwits, which was almost funny, all things considered.

The Americans, up close like this, had rather lost their film-star sheen. A lot of them didn't look much older than Sukie, and they were tired, jumpy, a bit bossy too, making it clear we weren't needed any more. It felt as if things were slipping away from us too fast.

Queenie glared at the colonel, unimpressed. 'What will happen to Mr Pengilly? The real Mr Pengilly, I mean, from the lighthouse?'

'Assuming he is the *real* Mr Pengilly,' he replied. 'The military police will speak to him as soon as possible, ma'am.'

I caught Esther's eye: she looked as troubled as I was.

'But he's getting married tomorrow afternoon to my sister,' I said.

'It's a security matter now, miss.' Colonel Bagatelli was unmoved. 'He'll be taken to Plymouth for questioning.'

Which was when I noticed how few soldiers were still here. They'd gone to arrest Ephraim, hadn't they? It was already too late.

'Are you taking my sister as well?' I asked, in panic. 'Because neither of them has done anything wrong.'

Out in the street – as if in answer, almost – a vehicle went past. Though we couldn't see it, I could tell from the rattly noise that it wasn't a normal motorcar but something bigger and rougher, like a truck. Another followed behind it, accelerating up the hill towards the main Plymouth road. I couldn't believe what was happening – and so quickly.

'What about Pixie?' Cliff was worried too. 'We can't leave her on her own.'

Mum put her arms around him, telling him to shush. Colonel Bagatelli had sense enough to see our distress, spreading his hands out like we were unpredictable animals he was trying to calm.

'Ladies, please, leave it to the experts. Go on inside, now. Have a cocoa, listen to something swell on the wireless. We'll know more in the morning. And,' he added, 'don't forget to lock the back door.'

'Whatever for?' Queenie scowled.

I was wondering the same thing. Was he expecting more Germans to wash up on the beach?

Apparently he was.

'We've had intelligence of an incursion planned for tonight,' he said. And from the way his grip tightened on the papers in his hands, I guessed where that *intelligence* had come from. I felt sick. 'Our dead man was carrying a map of a location just west of here along the coast. My men and I will be taking a little trip down there to check it out.'

So this was what the soldiers had been poring over.

'A map? Of where exactly?' I demanded.

'Olive!' Mum snapped. 'That's not your business!'

But it was all so frustrating. And I couldn't

understand why Mum was playing along with things, thanking the colonel graciously and taking Cliff inside, just like she'd been told to.

'She's picking her battles,' Esther whispered to me. 'You don't want her arrested as well, do you?'

True enough, I didn't. But I couldn't understand why no one was speaking up for Ephraim or Sukie.

'Come along, Olive,' Mum called over her shoulder. 'You'll have to sleep here tonight.'

Queenie, who clearly didn't think much of American soldiers or having her house invaded by us Bradshaws, followed with a sour look on her face.

'Are you coming in?' Esther asked me.

Wherever I went, I knew I'd be too churned up to sleep. No one had actually said that the wedding was off, but I couldn't for the life of me imagine how it could possibly be on. Reluctantly, I went inside.

A single soldier remained outside Queenie's back gate. I wasn't sure if he was protecting us or being our jailer, but he was instructed to stay there until morning.

'You're not driving any trucks, Johnson,' the colonel had said to him. 'Not after last time.' Whatever that meant.

Cliff, meanwhile, wouldn't shut up about Pixie.

'She's not used to being left on her own at the lighthouse,' he moaned. 'She'll be terrified.'

Mum tried to reassure him. 'At least she's somewhere she knows.'

If Sukie was here we'd have been *doing* something, I couldn't help thinking, not sitting around waiting for news from Plymouth. Mum seemed to guess what was on my mind. As we shuffled off to bed, she took me aside and told me, very firmly, not to do anything stupid.

'Your sister has a habit of courting trouble,' she said. 'But I'm trusting you to be sensible. Chances are they'll let them both go tomorrow. If we get involved, it could make matters worse.'

'The Americans found a map!' I reminded her. 'They're expecting more Nazis to come tonight. That already sounds pretty bad to me.'

'All the more reason to keep out of things you don't understand.'

'And what about the wedding?'

'It'll have to wait,' Mum replied. 'I can't help thinking Sukie's rushed into it, rather.'

'But Ephraim's innocent! He hasn't done anything wrong!'

'Olive.' Mum looked me square in the eye. 'If they

think Ephraim's helped the enemy, things will get *very* serious for him. I mean prison, spying charges. They might even accuse him of treason.'

I felt the blood drain from my face. '*Treason?* Isn't that a hanging offence?'

Mum didn't answer. 'I just don't want you getting mixed up in it, that's all.'

*

Esther had her own reasons for wanting to help Ephraim and, like me, didn't want to wait things out.

'What shall we do first?' I whispered, as we lay in bed pretending to be asleep.

'Check the German for papers,' she replied.

'But we already know what was in his pockets,' I pointed out. 'Everything had Ephraim's name on it, and the colonel's taken it all.'

'Ah, but they didn't take his bag. There might be hidden pockets in it.'

'Like with Sukie and Mum's coat,' I said, catching on. My sister had once smuggled a coded note inside the lining of a coat, so it was certainly worth checking if this man had done something similar.

'I want to show you another thing too. It's pretty

suspicious.' Esther swung her legs over the side of the bed. 'Coming?'

Mum's warning was still ringing in my ears as I pulled on my skirt and sweater and followed Esther down the steep attic stairs. It was no good waiting for the army to believe Ephraim. He wasn't the enemy. And what if there was an invasion tonight? We had to prove the dead German had stolen our friend's name, and we had until morning to do it.

6

The body lay exactly where the Americans had left him, in between Queenie's runner beans and the rhubarb.

'Look how dry the ground is here,' Esther hissed, pointing near our feet. 'It's very suspicious.'

Though with her torch already on the blink, it was hard to see what she was getting at.

'They rolled the body over, didn't they?' She sounded almost excited. 'If he'd drowned, his lungs would've been full of water. It would've leaked out as they moved him.'

Esther's dad was a doctor, so I supposed she was right.

'If he didn't drown, how did he die then?' I asked.

She glanced at the gate, on the other side of which Johnson the American was keeping guard. You could hear him out there, his leather boots creaking as he fidgeted into a more comfortable position.

'I don't know,' Esther whispered. 'But I'd guess he was dead before he even hit the water.'

I wasn't sure why she thought this so suspicious. Personally, I was more interested in the man's bag, which we were going to check for secret pockets. It had been easier to search him on the beach when I couldn't see his face. Now that he lay on his back, I glimpsed a snub nose, chapped lips, shaving stubble on a very square chin.

Quickly I turned my attention to the bag, which was cloth, like a kitbag, and completely wet through, with buckles on the front that my fingers couldn't get open at first. When it did open, a dead fish flopped out.

'Ugh!' I sprang back, stepping on Esther's foot.

She gasped out loud. 'Y-ouch!'

We both froze, terrified the guard had heard us. The gate stayed shut. Breathing again, I went back to my search. The bag appeared to be empty. When I felt the bottom part, though, there was a seam, and inside that seam a zip. It opened grittily, yank by yank. Inside was a leather wallet made stiff as a piece of slate by the sea. Stuffed in it were receipts, a train ticket, what could've been a shopping list. I sat back on my heels, stumped. It was all in German.

'I can read German,' Esther said, and took over.

She tipped the wallet upside down. In amongst the receipts was a black and white photograph, showing a boy about our age, standing in a garden. With his white-blond cropped hair and great square jaw, there was no question this was our dead man in his younger days. He was wearing what looked like a Scout uniform and smiling at the camera.

Esther shuddered, tapping the picture with her finger. 'That's the Hitler Youth uniform. Looks like he's been a Nazi for years.'

The wallet and photograph turned this dead body into a person who most definitely wasn't Ephraim Pengilly. There were receipts to say he'd bought things – bratwurst, which Esther told me was a type of German sausage, and cups of black coffee – all in Hamburg, Germany. It made the man seem more real than ever. We couldn't shrug it off as a mix-up. This man was *someone*. He even had a name, and that was our biggest problem.

Wearily, I rubbed my eyes. It was getting more complicated, not less.

'Won't our Ephraim have documents of his own?' I said. 'If we could find those—'

The back door opened. I froze, terrified it was Mum. But whoever it was slipped silently outside. I caught a flash of striped pyjamas darting between Queenie's gooseberry bushes.

'Cliff!' I whispered as loud as I dared.

He stopped, looking round for me.

'Over here!' I waved. 'Where are you going?'

But I'd already guessed: he was heading to the lighthouse. Every night he slept with Pixie at the foot of his bed, so no wonder he couldn't sleep without her. Esther and I got to our feet, brushing soil from our knees. I stuffed the German's wallet and receipts in my skirt pockets.

'We're coming with you,' I said. Though we'd have to tiptoe past the American first. I prayed Johnson had fallen asleep. The signs were encouraging because he'd gone awfully quiet. Yet when I eased open the gate, he stumbled inside like he'd been leaning up against it.

'Hell fire!' he cried, when he realised we weren't Nazis risen from the dead. 'What in God's name are you doing?'

We all spoke at once:

'Sleepwalking.'

'Getting some fresh air.'

'Sorting the dog out.'

One of these excuses *was* vaguely true, but we

sounded so totally suspicious it was no surprise that the soldier wouldn't let us pass.

'I've orders not to let anyone out or in,' he said, not unfairly. 'How about you go back to bed like good kids and we say no more about it, huh?'

None of us moved.

'So.' He sighed. 'We have a problem.' He pushed his army cap to the back of his head. I had a better glimpse of his face, then. He was dark-skinned, which, I'd imagine, got him a few looks from the locals. You didn't see many black people in Devon, not like London, where the mix made life that bit more interesting.

'Please, mister,' Cliff spoke first. 'There really *is* a dog. She belongs to the lighthouse keeper, and she's called Pixie. She's a fox terrier and honestly, she's the best dog in the—'

'Oh, spare us the details,' Esther groaned.

'Ephraim Pengilly is our friend,' I tried to explain. 'He's a kind man who wouldn't even swat a fly.' And because the soldier seemed a reasonable type, I half-wondered if I should come clean and explain that what we really wanted was Ephraim's birth certificate, a ration book, letters – anything to prove *he* was the real Mr Pengilly. Cliff could see to Pixie while we were there, a fact he was keen to remind us of.

'Mister, please,' Cliff kept on. 'It's not fair on Pixie, being shut in by herself. She'll be needing a wee by now.'

Esther groaned again.

Yet of all the things we'd said, Cliff's plea seemed to be working.

'A little terrier, you say, huh?' The young man's face softened. 'We had a dog like that back home in Boston. Called him Scout. Best ratter I ever saw, though he cried like a baby if he couldn't sleep in with me at night.'

'Exactly!' Cliff jumped at this – we all did. 'Pixie's just the same.'

'Jeez, I shouldn't let you go. I'm in the colonel's bad books already.' The soldier rubbed his jaw, weakening by the second.

'We'll be super quick,' Esther promised. 'And we'll bring Pixie back with us so you can meet her.'

Tapping his wristwatch, the soldier tried to look stern. 'No more than twenty minutes, got it? Or I'll come after you myself.'

'Yes, mister!' we all said at once.

'Kids, please,' he winced. 'My name's Eddie.'

He was, without doubt, the nicest American I'd ever spoken to. Actually, he was the only one, but still.

7

We ran down the main street to the harbour. By now the wind had dropped, so the night felt mild and calm. The sea was quiet, whispering and sighing over the shingle. Though we were more than used to climbing the lighthouse ladder these days, I still preferred to do it when the weather was gentle like this. I was nervous for other reasons tonight.

Just inside the front door Pixie was waiting, spinning around in circles.

'I'll take her down again,' Cliff said, hoisting her on to his shoulders like Ephraim had taught him to.

'Go straight back to Eddie,' I told him. 'Keep him entertained while we try and find Ephraim's papers.'

'Where first?' asked Esther, once Cliff and Pixie had gone.

'The top and work our way down?' I suggested.

Arming ourselves with a couple of the spare torches Ephraim left hanging by the front door, we climbed to the control room at the top of the lighthouse. It was a part of the building we normally kept away from, but I knew there was a desk up there, shelves, drawers, letters, maps, paperwork. It was a serious, grown-up sort of a room. If Ephraim had a passport, a birth certificate, documents from his parents perhaps, there was a good chance we'd find them up there.

Esther took the right-hand side of the room, I went left. I opened drawers, shook out folders, looked under books. I couldn't find anything that looked personal. On her side of the room, Esther also drew a blank.

'Nothing here,' she remarked. 'Perhaps he keeps private things separate? Like in his bedroom?'

'Good point,' I replied, thinking of how I'd once tried to hide things in my sock drawer. So had Sukie: fat lot of good it had done either of us. We'd both been rumbled.

I was also very aware of the minutes ticking away. Pixie might buy us a little extra time, but we couldn't count on it lasting.

Bypassing the living room and mine and Cliff's bedroom, we went straight back to where Ephraim slept. His was the floor just up from the lighthouse entrance. There was only one bed in it, a chest for clothes and piles upon piles of books, all stacked against the walls. Though the staircase took us through the room every time we came in and went out, I'd never paid much attention to it. Being here now felt like I was prying. Ephraim was such a private person – and why *was* that, the doubt-voice asked.

The sock drawer was, unsurprisingly, full of woolly socks. There was nothing under the bed, not even much in the way of dust. I was beginning to think we'd run out of places to look when I saw, in the far corner, a little cubbyhole in the wall. Had it been in the kitchen, I'd have thought it was a bread oven. There was an iron door on the front of it, stamped with BP, the lighthouse's initials.

'What d'you think it is?' I asked Esther as we crouched in front of it.

'Open it and find out,' she replied, practical as ever.

The door was unbelievably heavy, its hinges grinding like they'd not moved in years. Inside was a tin box with a little handle on the top of it. My first thought was money: this was where Ephraim kept his earnings. It was red, battered round the edges, the sort of box that might've seen a thing or two in its time.

I took out the tin box and opened it; there was no lock on it, no key. There was nothing inside, either. And by now I reckoned our twenty minutes of searching time must be well and truly up. Esther, though, had noticed something at the bottom of the box. She shone her torch right on to what looked like a small brass tack.

'Press it down,' she said.

As I did so something clicked and the base pinged upwards. Suddenly we were looking at an entirely different box, one that had a bundle of envelopes in it, and a card wallet with a name written across the front in fancy curled writing.

'Wow! A secret compartment!' I cried, then glanced at Esther. 'How did you know to press that button?'

'My nana had a box that was similar to this. She kept love letters in it from the man her parents didn't want her to marry.'

'I don't think these are love letters,' I said. Without picking them up I could see they were mostly documents.

'No,' Esther agreed. 'But they're something Ephraim wants to keep secret.'

'Like the pocket in the dead man's bag,' I muttered. It wasn't a comparison I wanted to make, but it was hard not to, suddenly. I was nervous that these papers might not prove Ephraim's innocence at all, but instead tell me something I really didn't want to read.

*

The first in the pile was a marriage certificate. On it were two names that I guessed were Ephraim's parents: his father's profession was 'lighthouse keeper', and his mother's 'schoolteacher'.

'Explains why he likes books so much,' I commented. 'And lighthouses.'

Esther pointed to another column, where the parents' names were. 'His father's surname was Prinz. That's a Jewish surname – a German one, I think.'

In with the marriage document was a boat ticket for a Josiah Prinz, and a stamp showing he'd arrived in Southampton from Hamburg in September 1920. It was a shock to discover Ephraim had German connections. I'd assumed Budmouth Point was in his bones, that his family had always lived here. Yet just a generation back and his father had left Germany as a young Jewish man.

I supposed Ephraim's dad had changed his name to an English one to fit in, just like Esther was given the surname Jenkins when she first arrived from Austria. No wonder, more than twenty years later, his son wanted to help refugees fleeing Hitler – I guessed that was in Ephraim's bones too.

'Does this make Ephraim Jewish?' I asked.

Esther shook her head. 'Not necessarily. It's passed on through the females in the family, but Ephraim's dad married someone non-Jewish, it looks like.'

Deeper in the pile was a birth certificate for Ephraim Josiah Pengilly. Born 24 April 1922 in this very lighthouse! Tucked in with it was something altogether sadder – a death notice for Mrs Roberta Katherine Pengilly, who, it seemed, died a day later.

'That's so *tragic*,' Esther said. 'To think he never knew his own mother.'

I nodded, blinking back tears, and stood up. Papers still in hand, I did a quick scan of the room. 'Is there anything else we might need from here?'

Out of the shore-side window, a light was flashing. It was coming from the beach. I was pretty certain it was Cliff, trying to warn us that Eddie the soldier was on his way. Why he hadn't gone straight to him like I'd told him to I didn't know.

'Come on, we'd better get going,' I said.

Esther scrambled to her feet. She stuck her hand out for Ephraim's papers. 'Shall I take those?'

I gave them to her, since my pockets were full with the dead German's wallet and receipts, and we couldn't afford to leave anything behind, or worse, drop something vital. Without the evidence it'd sound like a pack of lies.

We rushed down the final stairs to the front door. On opening it, I froze, my foot in mid-air. Down on the beach were *three* torches, not just one. It meant Cliff had company.

8

The moment I stepped on to the beach, a hand grabbed the scruff of my neck. I couldn't see who it was – everything was either torch-beam bright or very black – but they pulled so sharply backwards I almost lost my balance.

'Hey!' I yelped. 'No need to be so rough!'

'Don't hurt her,' Cliff pleaded.

Another person grabbed Esther. From the crunching of the shingle under her feet, I knew she was putting up a fight. We were frogmarched off the beach with such force I could actually hear my sweater ripping. I'd guessed by now Eddie was one of our captors, but I'd no idea who was holding me, and it was very unnerving.

Finally, up on the main street, the hand on my neck let go.

'Don't you *ever* go to bed?' said a voice I knew all too well.

In the dark, in front of me, stood Sukie.

'They let you go!' I gasped, though I didn't dare hug her. The anger was coming off her like steam.

'I didn't even get as far as Plymouth,' she replied. 'They asked me some questions, then gave up and brought me back.'

I couldn't understand: it was good news, wasn't it? The police must've believed her and Ephraim enough to let them come home. We wouldn't need these birth certificates and death notices to prove our point after all.

But Ephraim, I saw now, wasn't with her.

'Where is he?' I asked.

'In custody, of course! Where d'you think he is?' she snapped. 'They'd no intention of giving up on him.'

'But you're here,' I insisted. 'That's a start, isn't it?'

'And we've done some investigating,' Esther added, 'which we think should really help.'

'Does Mum know you're out here?' Sukie asked sharply.

'Umm, not exactly,' I admitted.

Sukie stuffed her hands in her trouser pockets. She was breathing hard through her nose like she was trying to calm down.

'I know you want to help, Olive,' she said, sounding bitter. 'But things are bad enough without you and your pals sticking your oar in.'

Esther tutted. 'Charming!'

'But we've got proof,' I insisted. 'That our Ephraim is the real one, with parents and a birth certificate. They'll be able to check all that out, won't they?'

'Not tonight,' Eddie cut in. 'Now, how about you make my life easier by going home to bed?'

*

Back at Queenie's, Mum was thrilled to see Sukie. It didn't last, mind you. Once Sukie told her where she'd found us, Mum blew her top.

'I blame *you*, Olive!' she cried, pointing a shaking finger right at me. I wanted to shrivel up on the spot. 'I expressly told you not to do anything stupid, didn't I?'

I nodded miserably.

'And taking your little brother along with you! In his pyjamas too! Where's your sense of responsibility?' she raged.

I glared at Cliff. He knew the truth, that we'd gone with him, not the other way round. But he looked so glum I kept quiet.

'I suppose you thought searching the lighthouse for Ephraim's paperwork was a good idea?' Mum asked.

'Actually, Mrs Bradshaw, we did,' Esther said, and

emptied her pockets on to the kitchen table. 'We found out Ephraim's father *was* German – a German Jew. But his mum was English, and she died a day after having him.'

Mum and Sukie both looked shocked. Esther's directness probably didn't cushion the blow.

'All it proves,' Mum pointed out, 'is that Ephraim has German connections. I'm not sure how that's going to help him.'

Yet pulling up a chair, Sukie started picking through the papers on the table. Her hands were shaking – all of her was.

'It'll come right, you'll see,' I said, sitting down next to her.

'Will it, Olive?' She looked completely out of her depth. And very, very scared.

Not knowing how to help, I took out the contents of my pockets too, and the table was soon covered in bits of scrunched-up paper, all claiming to be about the same person: Ephraim Pengilly. It was a complete and utter mess.

By Queenie's wall clock, the time was a little after one in the morning. There didn't seem much more we could do tonight.

'Bed,' Mum said, firmly.

Following Colonel Bagatelli's instructions, she tended to the back door, while Queenie saw to the front one. The sound of locks turning and bolts sliding made me think of poor Ephraim in his police cell. Just as we were leaving the kitchen, Pixie suddenly wanted to go out again.

'Uh-oh,' Cliff announced. 'She needs another piddle.'

I don't know why we all waited on the back doorstep for Pixie to do her business, but we did. At some point, we realised she'd been gone a rather long time.

'She'll have found a rat,' Cliff guessed. He called her, but she didn't come. What we could hear was the snuffling sound of a dog digging.

'My runner beans!' Queenie cried, and pushed past Mum.

We all knew what Pixie was like for digging. She'd burrow down to Australia if you left her to it. As the noises were coming from where the German lay, we followed Queenie outside. Sure enough, Pixie was digging at the dead man's pocket.

'Off, girl! Off!' Cliff cried, grabbing her by the collar.

Whatever she'd found was now sitting on the path. It was too dark to be certain what it was, but it looked small, with a long curly tail.

'Is it a rat? Has she killed it?' Cliff asked eagerly.

Esther picked it up, which was mightily brave considering she didn't like rats.

'It's not a rat,' she said, turning it over in her hand. 'It's a radio.'

Which proved everything. In a flash.

All that climbing ladders and searching secret boxes, and here was the best piece of evidence of all.

'He's been passing on information!' I cried, though Esther, holding the radio by its loose wire, indicated it was as dead as the German who'd been carrying it. 'Or that's what he was planning!'

'He's a spy, then!' Cliff chipped in. 'He must be!'

'I thought as much,' Queenie said.

Sukie took a huge, relieved breath.

If anything could prove our Ephraim's innocence, then surely this was it. All the other parts of this queer set-up began to take on new meanings.

'That's why they named the German Ephraim Pengilly,' I said, working it out as I spoke. 'So the authorities would get suspicious of the real Ephraim, and take him away. A lighthouse without a lighthouse keeper—'

'Makes it easier to land something on the beach,' Esther agreed. 'And you know what I said about the German not having drowned?'

I did.

'I bet he was already dead when they threw him in the water. They dressed him up, gave him a bag and a made-up name.'

'But where did they get Ephraim's name from?' Cliff asked.

'Hamburg, I guess.' Esther told him. 'This man came from Hamburg and so did Ephraim's father. That's probably the link.'

'So really he's just a decoy to throw us off the scent.' I added.

'And a listening device too,' Queenie agreed. 'This is a classic case of misinformation. It's an intelligence tactic used to confuse the enemy.'

Before she could say any more the gate swung open. Behind it was the broad outline of Eddie.

'Now come on, you guys,' he said, sounding a little fed up. 'Either that cute dog has got a bathroom problem or you're just playing around here. Get yourselves inside, like the colonel said.'

None of us moved.

'Are we going to tell him?' Queenie asked.

'Tell me what?' he wanted to know.

There was a tense pause before Queenie cleared her throat. 'This is all fake: the man, the papers, the set-up, it's just a ruse to misinform us.'

That wasn't the worst of it, either, I realised with growing dread.

'That map the German was carrying,' I said. 'The one showing where the incursion is meant to be happening just down the coast – where all your soldier chums have gone – it's a fake! It's *all* a fake!'

'*What?*' Eddie stiffened. 'But that map showed the exact place – to the west of the lighthouse. I saw it myself!'

I'd been expecting Mum would tell me to be quiet, but now she moved to stand beside me. 'Olive's right. So's Queenie. It's all a set-up to make sure this bit of coast is clear of anyone on lookout.'

'So if they're not landing to the west of the lighthouse, where *are* the Nazis coming?' Esther asked, bewildered.

'It must be near here. Near the lighthouse,' Queenie said.

'Could it be like a code?' I suggested. 'They might've told us opposites. The west of Budmouth could actually be the east.'

In other words, the next cove along: Tythe Cove.

If I was right, it also meant Eddie was the only soldier for miles around.

No soldiers, no lighthouse keeper – exactly as the Germans wanted it. And now they were coming, with just us here to stop them.

9

Eddie told us to find a weapon. I grabbed a rake, Esther took a spade. Mum and Queenie both seized axes from the woodshed. Cliff was given a rolling pin. And, just like she'd promised a few weeks ago, Sukie carried a garden fork.

Seven people weren't an army, though. So while Queenie went to rouse Mrs Henderson, who had the keys to the church bell tower, the rest of us ran through the village knocking on doors and shouting through letter boxes.

'Wake up! You're needed!'

'Emergency!'

'The Germans are coming!'

We raced up and down the main street, then along by the school, and as far as Salters Cottages at the very top of the village. The church bells were ringing. Just as I'd thought it'd be, the sound was horrible – so jarring and out of place. It was like hearing the air-raid

A gasp of shock went through the crowd. Then shouts of 'Shame on Jerry!' and 'Well, I never!' and 'For crying out loud! As if!' No one believed Ephraim would be involved, not for a second.

'What are we waiting for?' someone said. 'Let's get cracking!'

The crowd started forwards.

'Wait!' Queenie held up her hands. 'We go quietly, please. In single file along the cliff path. When we get to Tythe Cove, we watch and we listen.'

*

The path up over the headland was narrow at the best of times. Now, in the dark, with fog swirling around us, it was hard to know where to put your feet. We were a long thin line stretching along the clifftop, Queenie and Eddie in front, Mrs Henderson in the middle somewhere, Mum and Sukie bringing up the rear.

'Keep an eye on your brother, Olive,' Mum said to me.

We made good progress at first, passing the pillbox where tonight's Home Guard on lookout was Mr Fairweather, a local farmer. He left his flask of tea to join us.

'Can't see nothing in this fog, anyhow,' he remarked. 'You youngsters have got better eyes.'

After the pillbox, the path got steeper. I made Cliff walk in front of me with Pixie on a short leash. Esther was right behind. Every now and then as she stumbled on a loose stone, I'd spin round to check she was still there.

'Jeez, Olive, stop fussing!' Esther said crossly, when it happened for about the fifth time.

As I faced forwards again, the stumbling noises now came from up ahead.

'Oh!' someone cried, almost in surprise.

Craning my neck I could just about see Queenie. My heart skipped a beat.

Our line of people bumped to a halt. She was crouched at the cliff edge, holding a person's hands.

Someone who'd gone over.

In a panic I ran straight to her, dragging Cliff with me.

'He slipped,' Queenie gasped. 'I've nearly got him.'

She hadn't. In fact, she was losing her grip. Two huge straining hands struggled to keep hold of her little birdlike ones. It was never going to work.

Over the edge, I glimpsed Eddie's grimacing face. I grabbed his arm at the elbow. On the opposite side,

Cliff did the same. Esther took hold of Queenie by the waist. Other people were now crowding round, grabbing hold and shouting encouragement. On the count of three this time, we pulled together. It took everything we had, but as we all tumbled back into the gorse bushes, Eddie came with us.

There were cheers. A laugh of relief. Queenie sat up, breathless, then surprised me by giving Eddie a very quick, very strong hug.

'Don't do it again,' she said, as she got to her feet.

Eddie stood up, looking rather embarrassed.

*

When we set off again, we went slower, and on trembling legs. The sea fog was thicker than before. It was wet, and cold, soaking through my cardigan and making my skirt stick unpleasantly to my knees. And then, quite suddenly, we came to a stile. Either side of it were rolls of barbed wire, and beyond the steep steps cut into the hillside that took you down on to the little horseshoe-shaped beach of Tythe Cove.

Normally from this spot you could see for miles. It was where Ephraim came last year when the boat he'd been expecting from France had seemed so late. Even in darkness, on a good night, you'd be able to see what was out on the water. Tonight, you couldn't even tell what was ground and what was thin air: the fog had put paid to that.

Queenie went first over the stile. Then Eddie. We followed behind. By the time we reached the beach, my thigh muscles were burning from the climb down. It was impossible to walk quietly on the shingle, though we all tried.

Finally, when the last person was on the beach, a silence settled over us. And that quiet – that listening – was all we had to go by, as the fog swallowed us up. Reaching out, I squeezed Esther's hand. She squeezed back. Cliff leaned against me, just for a second.

I hardly breathed, I was listening so hard. But the fog muffled things, made sounds seem different, so it was difficult to know what was what.

Still, I knew the crackle of a radio when I heard it. I also knew what German sounded like. The voice came out of nowhere, making me freeze in terror.

10

'What the blazes?' cried Mrs Henderson.

Everyone flew into action. But we were bumbling blind, knocking arms, shovels, treading on each other's feet. The German voice was close. Very close. It was, we realised, coming from Esther's coat pocket, where she still had the dead spy's radio.

'Crikey! It's working again!' She was as startled as anyone.

'What's it saying?' This was Mrs Henderson. 'Shh! Can we listen?'

There was a rustle as Esther took the radio from her pocket. The hissing, crackling noise grew louder. The same clipped flat voice that sent a chill down my neck spoke again, this time in English:

'*We proceed to the shore.*'

I stared at the thing in Esther's hand, almost wishing it *was* a rat. 'They're out there, aren't they?'

'Sounds like it,' Eddie agreed.

Queenie gestured that we should spread out in a line again. The message went quickly through the group. We stood, weapons ready, facing the ocean – or at least at the bank of fog where the ocean was meant to be. Straight ahead, you could hear the quiet lapping of the sea. We waited, ears straining. A minute went by. Then another.

Mum touched my shoulder.

'I know I'm usually telling you to keep your nose out of things,' she whispered. 'But I'm proud of you, Olive. If only your dad could see you now.'

I was halfway to a smile when someone cried out: 'Oh lord alive, there's a BOAT!'

How they knew I'd no idea. And not being able to see it felt *more* frightening, somehow. In my mind's eye it was a huge great battleship with machine guns trained on us, like those ones you saw on newsreels at the cinema, the hull part would open out and tanks roll on to our beach. I felt weak with fear.

Queenie hissed for us to all shut up. Weapons at the ready, we went still again. The swishing, sloshing sound was faint at first. I thought it might be the tide. There was a rhythm to it, though, and quickly I twigged it was the noise of oars moving through the water.

A rowing boat? Hitler's men were trying to invade the British Isles in a *rowing* boat?

It was almost funny. Yet despite the relief that we probably weren't about to be gunned down, I was angry too. Did the Nazis really think we'd give in that easily?

The boat was coming closer to the shore. Or it seemed to be. *Swoosh-drip, swoosh-drip*: my ears stayed trained on the noise. Either side of me, Esther and Mum were poised, ready. I tightened my grip on the garden rake. And just when I expected to see the boat at last, the swooshing grew fainter. Then it died away completely.

We were back to the creepy silence again. Even the radio seemed to have given up the ghost.

'What do we do now?' Esther asked.

'Nobody move,' Queenie replied. 'Be ready if they attack.'

'But they're not there, love,' Mrs Drummond from the bakery pointed out. 'Perhaps they never were. It might've been a fishing boat all along.'

'Oh no,' Esther countered. 'You heard the radio just now.'

'And the dead German in Queenie's garden,' said Cliff. 'He's not come to Devon for a holiday, has he?'

From the direction of the sea came a faint sploshing sound. Then another.

'D'you hear that?' I hissed. 'It's them again! They're back!'

Mrs Drummond sighed. 'It's the *sound* of a boat, Olive, my dear. How on earth do we fight a noise?'

She was right, of course. We couldn't see a boat, but we could *hear* one, and it was terrifying. I remembered something from school about how the Ancient Britons did battle with the Romans, when they knew they were massively outnumbered and didn't stand a chance. If your enemy couldn't see you, you tricked them. You made them *think* you were powerful, making a heck of a lot of noise. It was misinformation of a sort.

'We're going to fight back with *our* noise,' I said, because it stood as much chance of scaring off the enemy as a stupid garden rake.

'Now, miss.' This was Eddie, who'd been quiet until this point. 'I can't say that's a swell—'

The sloshing was getting louder again. There wasn't time to argue. I shouted into the fog: 'WE HAVE WEAPONS! I WARN YOU!'

The oar-noise kept coming.

'THE POLICE ARE ALL ALONG THE BEACH HERE!' Queenie yelled. 'TAKE ONE STEP ON TO

BRITISH SOIL AND YOU WILL BE ARRESTED ON SIGHT!'

Out in the fog, someone coughed. The rowing slowed, then started again in earnest.

'THIS IS OUR HOME!' Esther yelled. 'AND WE'RE NOT AFRAID TO PROTECT IT!'

'JUST TRY IT! OUR WEAPONS ARE SHARP AND AT THE READY, AND BE WARNED, WE'VE GOT SPIFFINGLY GOOD AIM!' Sukie hollered.

'WE HAVE YOUR MAN AND HIS RADIO!' Mum added. 'WE KNOW EXACTLY WHAT YOU'RE UP TO!'

Now Eddie joined in. 'AND DON'T THINK OF TRYING YOUR LUCK FURTHER DOWN THE COAST, *PALS*. THE AMERICAN ARMY HAVE GOT DEVON COVERED!'

I held my breath, hoping we'd scared them just enough to make them think twice about coming ashore. But the boat sounded closer than ever.

'Oh heck,' I muttered. 'They're still coming.'

'AND WE HAVE A FEROCIOUS GUARD DOG!' Cliff bellowed. 'WHO WE'RE LETTING LOOSE RIGHT AT THIS MOMENT ...'

Pixie did her biggest, gruffest bark, then raced down

the beach. We heard a curse in German, a scrabble in the water, and then the sound of a boat quickly rowing away.

We waited. We listened. Pixie padded back up the beach, her tongue lolling, tail wagging. The boat, though, didn't return.

*

Only one person complained when, the next morning, Budmouth Point's post office and shops were all late to open. We were woken by him pummelling on Queenie's front door, and for someone with such small fists, he was terrifically loud.

'Good grief, woman!' Mr Spratt fumed. 'What on earth's going on? Has the whole village died since yesterday?'

Queenie, who'd stumbled to the door in her dressing gown, didn't invite him inside. We heard everything from Esther, who'd sat on the stairs to listen in.

'Last night we faced an enemy invasion.' Queenie was chilly, to say the least. 'You were needed here, Mr Spratt, yet you didn't come.'

'An enemy invasion? What tommyrot!' he blustered. 'The message I received mentioned a body, nothing else.'

'Anyway, we dealt with it,' Queenie told him.

Mr Spratt laughed in disbelief. '*You?* Dealt with an invasion? That's the funniest thing I've heard in some time!'

Queenie didn't *exactly* shut the door in his face, but Esther said it wasn't far off.

Though I couldn't ever see myself agreeing with Mr Spratt, it *did* sound a bit of a tall story: us scaring off a boat full of Nazi soldiers with only garden implements and Pixie as weapons. But it *had* happened, hadn't it? Pretty much all of Budmouth Point was witness to the fact.

As we went into the kitchen to make tea, there was no sign of Sukie. When Cliff let Pixie out into the backyard, he came back saying the dead German had vanished too. I wasn't sure if this was good news or bad. Things still felt very much up in the air and would do until Ephraim came home.

The Americans had taken the body, we soon found out. And when Mrs Henderson arrived, we heard about Sukie's movements too.

'I saw that sister of yours on the back of some soldier's motorcycle,' Mrs Henderson said to me as we stood at the stove frying bread and eggs for breakfast. 'First light, it was, as I went to milk the goats.'

'A motorcycle?' Mum looked up from her tea.

'Would that be Eddie's?'

'Might be,' I said, thinking how daring it sounded. 'He's not allowed to drive a van.'

'Which direction was she heading in?'

'Out of the village on the Plymouth road. Going like the wind, they were,' Mrs Henderson replied.

'And she's taken the German radio and all Ephraim's papers,' Esther confirmed after getting up to search her coat pockets.

My heart gave a little skip. I caught Mum's eye. Things were definitely looking up. 'You don't suppose, if they let Ephraim go—'

Mum glanced at the clock. 'It's nine o'clock now. The church is booked for two.' She blew out a breath. 'They'll be cutting it fine.'

'But it's possible?' I pressed.

Mum smiled. 'You know your sister, Olive. Anything's possible.'

11

Yet even Sukie couldn't make three people fit on one motorcycle. When they *did* return, it was in slightly less glamorous style on the lunchtime bus. Cliff and me, ever hopeful, had been on lookout since breakfast, so the sight of Sukie and Ephraim coming in through Queenie's side gate made us rush out, squealing. And even then, Pixie still reached them first.

There wasn't time for explanations. By now it was gone one o'clock. Mum, taking Sukie's hand, whisked her off upstairs to get ready. For someone who just two days ago had wanted the wedding plans to slow down, I was relieved at how fast she was moving now.

'Olive, Esther!' Mum called over her shoulder. 'Hurry up! Come and get changed!'

Esther, giggling excitedly, bounded up the stairs after them. I didn't follow straight away. In the kitchen still was Ephraim, who was about to return to the lighthouse with Cliff. Seeing him now felt different,

162

somehow. I supposed it was because I knew a little more about him – about his parents, his Jewishness, his never having known his mum. Yet in amongst it all he was still the same quiet, gentle Ephraim, and the least likely German spy I ever saw.

'I'm glad you're back,' I said.

'So am I.' He frowned a little. 'Though I'm not sure I should thank you for going through my private things.'

'I'm sorry,' I replied, blushing. 'But it helped in the end, didn't it?'

He smiled. There were tears in his eyes. 'What helps more than anything is being part of a family again.' He opened his arms and I went to him. And that hug – in that moment – was as good as any from my dad. I hoped Ephraim felt better for it too.

*

By two o'clock the little church was full to bursting. In the front pew were Queenie, Mrs Henderson, Esther and me. Behind us were Jim, Mrs Drummond, the local teacher, Mrs Simmons, and on it went, with those who couldn't squeeze in spilling out into the churchyard and the lane beyond. Amongst the summer hats and printed frocks were the khaki-clad

Americans. They'd come back from Plymouth, rather baffled by the dead German's maps.

'It was misinformation,' I heard Queenie trying to explain to Colonel Bagatelli before we went in. 'They tried to land here, to the east.'

Yet though the colonel was more courteous than Mr Spratt had been, I could tell he didn't quite believe Queenie's version of events, either.

'Do you have proof of that, ma'am?' he asked. 'I'd be very interested to see.'

But proof was the one thing we didn't have. We couldn't even describe what the Germans looked like. All we had to go on was our word.

Meanwhile, only one of the Americans was invited inside the church and that was Eddie, who was so tall he could hardly fit his long legs into the pew.

'Look at Queenie,' Esther whispered, as Eddie sat behind her.

I already had a hunch about Queenie and Eddie. The smile on her face, the way she'd pinned her hair and worn an actual dress for once, confirmed it.

'Good for her,' I said happily.

The church organ started up then, and turning in our seats, we saw Cliff coming inside with Ephraim, who was nervously smoothing his hair. He was in his best suit and tie, wearing a white rosebud in his buttonhole. Taking his place at the altar, he flashed us a quick smile.

'Good luck!' I mouthed.

'Break a leg!' Esther whispered, loud enough for all the front row to hear.

Sukie came in next, beaming, on Mum's arm.

'Oh my word!' Esther gasped. 'She looks like Ava Gardner!'

I'd always thought my sister was magnificent, but I'd have bet even Ava Gardner wouldn't look this beautiful in a dress made out of curtains. No offence to Esther, but she and I certainly didn't carry off the pale yellow brocade in the same way.

'She looks incredible,' I sighed.

To save fabric, the dress fell only just below Sukie's knee. The waist was nipped in, the neckline what Mrs Henderson called a 'sweetheart', and at the side were gorgeous little glass buttons that Queenie had paid for with her clothing coupons. On her head, she wore summer flowers in a band that Esther had made.

'Nothing's going to top that outfit,' Esther remarked.

Though pretty quickly she had to eat her words.

'Bring 'em here!' Cliff called out, and Pixie bounded down the aisle, carrying a little basket in her mouth.

Though she stopped for a quick sniff of someone's

shoe, when she reached Cliff she lay perfectly at his feet. Inside the basket, nestled in hay, you could just about see two gold rings, glinting. Ephraim looked overjoyed. Sukie laughed. And Cliff was as pleased as punch. Before, on the beach when he'd showed me the trick, well, let's just say it hadn't gone to plan. Thankfully now, when it mattered, it worked.

*

Later, we had afternoon tea at the village hall. Last spring we'd had another party here to welcome our Jewish friends to England. Today we were celebrating similar things – friendship, family, hope, and, if you were Cliff and me, how much food you could fit on your plate in one go. The goat butter wedding cake wasn't actually too bad. Inside its rice-paper covering, it was smaller than it first looked, and the currants were really chopped-up prunes from a tin. But it was cake, so no one minded. Besides, there was plenty else on offer thanks to people pooling their rations – spam sandwiches, jam tarts, hard-boiled eggs from Mrs Simmons's chickens, and everyone's favourite, carrot fudge.

Later still, as the party went on into the evening and teapots were swapped for jugs of cider, Esther, Cliff and me took a stroll down to the sea. Pixie had refused to come. She was suddenly glued to Ephraim's side again, which made Cliff a bit sad I could tell.

Instead of staying on Budmouth beach, we took the path over the clifftops to Tythe Cove. In the fading sunlight, it was a pretty walk now the fog had cleared away, with splendid views out over the sea and along the coast towards Salcombe. Down on the beach itself it was quiet, and when we found a spot to sit, the shingle still felt warm through my frock.

'I wish I had a dog,' Cliff said to no one in particular.

'I'm sure Pixie still loves you,' I told him.

He hugged his knees. 'It's not the same as having your own, though, is it?'

'I s'pose not.'

Thankfully, Esther changed the subject. 'Funny how the weather changes so fast along this coast. It's like another world down here today.'

She was quiet – dreamy almost – as she sat, skimming stones out across the water. It was a side of Esther most people never saw, and made her even more dear to me.

'That's one of the reasons why Budmouth Point has a lighthouse, so Ephraim says,' I replied. 'It's not an easy place for boats to navigate.'

'Can't say I'd try it, if I was a Nazi,' said Cliff.

'Mr Spratt and Colonel Bagatelli don't believe they actually did,' Esther commented, then suddenly sat up straight. 'Hey! That was a fantastic skim! It bounced four times!'

'Show-off,' Cliff muttered.

To be honest, I wasn't even looking. I'd spotted something red and gold down at the water's edge. A bit of rubbish, that's what it looked like, sopping wet and all scrunched up. Getting to my feet, I went over, picked it up, smoothed it out a little. It was a chocolate wrapper.

A German chocolate wrapper.

Racing back up the beach, I showed the others.

'Look!' I cried. 'There were Germans here last night!'

Cliff whooped, stared, then passed it to Esther, who held it at arm's length like it was dirt.

'I can't wait to see the look on Mr Spratt's face when we show him,' she said triumphantly.

'Maybe.'

Personally, I wasn't so sure we needed to: we all knew what we'd done. We'd heard those church bells ringing and been ready. We'd been our own little army. We'd seen off the Nazis, and we'd found out the truth about the drowned man. I'd say that wasn't bad for an evening's work. We didn't have to prove anything to Mr Spratt: what mattered was we'd proved it to ourselves.

OPERATION
GREYHOUND

1

Velvet Jones hated air raids. They made her feel like a coconut in a shy at the fair, just sitting there waiting to be smashed to smithereens. Not that there was much left of Plymouth to bomb any more, but the Luftwaffe kept coming – she'd lost track of how many times. In the city centre the one shop left standing was Marks and Spencer, and only because it was propped up with poles.

The worst thing about air raids was the noise – the siren, the deadweight drone of planes, the terrific *whump* you felt through the soles of your feet when a bomb hit its target.

'Doesn't Hitler *ever* have a day off?' Velvet groaned as, just after tea that evening, the siren sounded yet again.

'No and nor do I, thanks to him,' Mrs Jones replied. Her mum worked nights as a firewatcher, putting out incendiaries dropped by German planes. She'd been asleep when the siren went off – Velvet could tell from the bad-tempered look on her face. 'Go on, then, get yourself up to the shelter, Vee!'

Mrs Jones had called her daughter Velvet precisely because her dad had begged her not to, and when he'd sailed home to St Lucia, she'd been stuck with an angry mother and a stupid name. 'Vee' wasn't much better, though her mum seemed to find it easier to say with force.

So Velvet grabbed her gas mask, her cardigan, a book. With a mum who worked all hours, she was used to looking after herself.

*

Barton Street, where the Joneses lived, stood a couple of streets back from the quayside. The houses were mostly little two-up-two-downs, with front doors that opened straight out on to the pavement, and windows that were permanently blurred with sea salt. It was once where the fishermen and sailors had lived when their feet touched dry land.

Out in the street as the air-raid siren wailed, people weren't exactly rushing for the public shelter. It was more of a grim, resigned plod up the hill because this was the third raid in a week, and everyone was tired.

Some were still in their housecoats, or swallowing a last mouthful of supper. Like Velvet, most of the children hadn't yet changed out of their school clothes.

On the opposite side of the road, she spotted her best friend, Lynn.

'Hey, wait for me!' she called, running over to where Lynn was dragging her dog up the street.

Lynn wanted to be a vet when she was older. Where Velvet had a tendency to get in a flap about things, Lynn was quite sensible, with the look of a person who made constant lists in her head. But tonight she was having real trouble with her terrified dog, Sprout. He hated air raids too.

It was the same for lots of animals. Some people reckoned their pets could sense the planes before the sirens even started. Together, with a combination of more pulling and the biscuit crumbs from Velvet's pocket, they somehow got Sprout up the hill.

'Don't worry, Sprouty,' Velvet told him, crouching down to tickle his chin. 'The raid'll soon be over.'

Lynn grimaced. 'I hope you're right. Poor Mum's dead on her feet.' Mrs Parsloe, Lynn's mother, also worked nights – in her case driving an ambulance – and came home each morning so dirty and exhausted she often fell asleep in the bath. Lynn's father was away fighting in Egypt, somewhere. Occasionally, he'd send home photos of himself with a sunburnt nose.

At the steps down to the public shelter, a straggly queue was forming – of people with dogs, cats and numerous baskets, boxes, bulging bags inside which were smaller creatures of the furry and feathery kind. Luckily, the residents of Barton Street had an understanding warden called Mr Perks, who let them bring their pets to the shelter.

'Can't leave the little blighters at home alone, can we, eh?' he'd say, and lead his own old brindle bull terrier, Nipper, into the shelter to make himself comfortable on someone's lap. It meant the shelter was more cramped, smellier and noisier than ever. And Nipper was a great lump of a thing. But for Velvet, who loved animals, it made the long nights almost bearable. Other people's pets were the next best thing to having your own.

'Busy tonight,' said Betty, who ran the pub on the corner of their street.

Mrs Gable from number six shifted her box of hens on to her other hip. 'It's them lot from Portland Place,' she said knowingly. 'They're bombed out, aren't they? Can't even use their own shelters, poor devils.'

Portland Place was a couple of roads away. The houses there were bigger and had gardens in which most people had their own Anderson shelter. At least they did until last week, when a bomb took out half the street.

Just like the animal lovers of Barton Street, the Portland Place people had brought their pets with them. There were almost more cats and dogs than people in the queue, which to Velvet's mind was no bad thing.

'What's this I hear about a new air-raid warden starting tonight?' Mrs Gable was saying now.

'A new one?' Velvet asked. 'What's happened to Mr Perks?' Though it was Nipper she was really thinking about. On recent nights, he'd chosen her lap to sleep on, and it was ever so comforting when the bombing got too much.

Mrs Gable glared at her: even on Barton Street kids didn't butt in on grown-up conversations. But Betty was friendlier. 'He's gone to his sister's on Dartmoor, love. He's worn out, poor chap, what with all these raids. Said he needed some country air.'

'He was looking peaky, Betty,' Mrs Gable agreed. 'And coughing something rotten, which never bodes well.'

The thought of no Nipper tonight made Velvet glum.

'This new warden,' Betty went on, 'calls himself

Mr Jackson and he's already told Mr Khan to make sure we sit in house number order.'

Lynn, who liked things to be organised, looked almost impressed. Then, seeing Velvet's face, she said, 'Sounds a bit like school.'

'Well, it *is* school,' Velvet reminded her, because the shelter itself was deep in the cellars under their school, and the man whose job it was to enforce the air-raid warden's rules was their head teacher, Mr Khan.

*

Down in the shelter, people crammed on to the benches that ran along either side, and when they were full up, sat on the floor. The new rule about sitting in house number order wasn't going down well.

'It's quite simple, Mrs Gable,' Mr Khan said, trying to keep his temper. 'You're number six so you should sit next to number seven.'

'But all the odds are on one side of the street,' she protested, 'and all the evens on the other. So that's not the right order.'

In the end, just to get everyone inside and the door shut behind them, the new rule was abandoned. Velvet sat cross-legged on the clammy brick floor, with Lynn on her left, and Mo, her other best pal, on her right. There were elbows, feet, dogs, baskets and boxes everywhere, and with it a weary sense of business as usual. Lanterns were lit, flasks of tea poured. People got out their books, knitting, packs of cards, peppermints.

Overhead, the German planes had already arrived. The sound was horrid – a slow, never-ending rumble that made Velvet's eardrums ache. She would've rather liked to hold Lynn's hand, but her friend was busy rocking Sprout like a baby. Times like these she wished she had a dog of her own to hug. Or at least Nipper, who despite being ancient had fur that smelled like butter. But her mum always said pets were too much responsibility.

'I've enough worry looking after you,' she'd say, which Velvet thought was a bit rich when most of the time she was either asleep or working. These days Velvet had to wash her own clothes and cook her own suppers, both with limited success.

Inside a box near Velvet's feet, someone's cat had started yowling as if it was about to be sick. A few of the shelter dogs were panting and whimpering. Though some had got used to the raids these past weeks others, like Sprout, still got horribly frightened.

'Shh there, silly, it's all right,' she said, trying her best to soothe the animals near enough to hear. Though by now her own nerves were welling up. Being surrounded by animals didn't seem to be helping tonight.

She turned to Mo. 'You think it's going to be a heavy raid?'

'Hmm?' He didn't look up from his book, which was typical. Mo – short for Mohammed – lived two doors down from Velvet. He'd come to England with his parents a couple of years ago from a city called Lahore in India, where people were fighting a war of their own over which country they should belong to, and other things Velvet didn't understand.

'The raid? D'you think—' Velvet was distracted by a movement in Mo's jacket pocket, as a small pink rodent-sized nose appeared. Mo's pet rat, Sherlock, was super intelligent, and super sweet. 'I'd get more sense out of you, wouldn't I?' she murmured, stroking his silky whiskers.

There was a sudden sharp knock at the shelter door, and Sherlock ducked back into Mo's pocket. The whole shelter went quiet.

'D'you think it's *him*?' someone whispered.

'What, the new air-raid warden?' This was Mo's mother, Mrs Hussein.

'Who else could it be, Mum?' Mo muttered. No one went out in an air raid for the fun of it.

Murmurs spread along the benches. Should they move seats? Should they organise themselves into house number order? Would Mr Khan get into trouble if they didn't?

The knock came again, louder and more frantic. Mr Khan stood up. Turning to everyone, he put a finger to his lips.

'Not a word about the seats!' he hissed.

He lifted the black curtain slightly, edging open the door.

'I thought you were never going to let us in!' The voice was a woman's.

Before Mr Khan could reply, she'd shouldered her way inside. She was shivering in a flimsy summer frock and sandals. With her was a boy and a scruffy dog. Velvet recognised him instantly.

'Don't tell me that's the new air-raid warden,' Mo whispered.

'Of course it isn't,' Velvet replied.

It was someone far more interesting.

2

The boy's name was Robert Clements. Last week, on a rare day when Velvet's mum hadn't been asleep, they'd been out shopping when the boy stepped right into their path.

'Thank you,' he'd said, staring at Mrs Jones. 'For what you did last night. Thank you.'

Her mum never talked about what happened on her night shifts. And Velvet never asked. She knew it must be grim, though, and the look of almost panic on her mother's face confirmed that she really didn't want to be speaking about it here, in the middle of the street.

'That's all right, chum,' she'd said and kept walking.

Afterwards, Mrs Jones told her just enough: the boy was called Robert, and he lived with his mother – a Mrs Clements – on Portland Place. An incendiary had fallen in their back garden, setting fire to their shed. They'd got off lightly compared to some of their neighbours who'd been badly bombed.

'All I did was bang on their front door to tell them,' she explained. 'You'd think I'd fought off the Germans single-handed from how grateful he was.'

But the boy's face had been so full of hero-worship, it left Velvet wondering whether there was more to her bossy, practical, overall-wearing mother than met the eye.

And now here was the boy again, this time with a dog in tow, looking far less excitable than he had that day in the street. He was dark-haired, pale-cheeked and wearing the grammar school's uniform: Velvet noticed the black and yellow wasp-striped tie around his neck. His mother, in her summer dress, smiled politely at all the faces turned their way. It was odd how no one smiled back.

'Do the door then, son!' Mr Khan instructed.

Robert stood on tiptoe to pull the blackout blanket across the doorframe. When he'd finished, everyone was asked to shuffle along the bench so he and his mother could sit down. Reluctantly, people moved, making just enough room for one small person. 'Thank you, you're very kind,' Mrs Clements said, sliding into the space. Hers wasn't a Barton Street accent, or even a Plymouth one. And yet from the frosty reaction, everyone seemed to know who she was.

Robert remained on his feet.

'Sit with us if you like.' Velvet patted a spot nearby

on the floor. She was, she decided, going to ask him about the night with the incendiary. She also rather liked the look of his dog.

'I'll stand, thanks,' he muttered, gesturing to his dog. 'She's a bit funny with dogs she doesn't know.'

The dog was whippet-sized but hairy, with a round belly and very skinny legs.

'She's pregnant!' Lynn whispered excitedly in Velvet's ear.

'Is she?' Velvet didn't question how her friend could tell. Lynn knew more about animals than all the *Encyclopaedia Britannica*s put together.

'No, Sprout, stop sniffing,' Lynn tutted, because he was interested too and was nosing his way through people's legs to reach Robert's dog.

He'd almost made it when another pounding on the shelter door made everyone jump.

'YOU IN THERE! YOUR LIGHTS ARE SHOWING!'

There was no mistaking the authority of the person shouting. It was the new air-raid warden, Mr Jackson.

'Uh-oh,' Betty from the pub groaned. 'We're for it now.'

Robert, as the last person in, was supposed to have secured the door. The boy looked so uncomfortable Velvet felt rather sorry for him. The fine for showing light in a blackout could be as much as £20.

'OPEN UP AT ONCE!' the warden demanded.

And so, with a weary sigh, Mr Khan opened the door. The man who squeezed inside was short: the top of his tin helmet didn't quite reach Mr Khan's shoulder. He had a sharp face, the chin made even sharper by a very pale, very pointy beard.

'Ferret-face,' Mo said under his breath. Velvet had to pinch her nose to stop the nervous giggle that was threatening to turn into a snort.

'You seem very full tonight, Mr Khan,' Mr Jackson observed. When he shone his torch into the corners and down at the floor, he got a big surprise. 'It's like a ruddy zoo down here!'

It was true: the shelter *was* crammed. People were squashed together like pilchards in a tin. And coming in from outside as Mr Jackson had, he must've noticed how the air reeked of pipe smoke, hair oil, beer – and, of course, animals.

Mr Khan straightened his shoulders. 'What do you expect us to do about it now?'

Whatever Mr Jackson was about to say was lost in a terrific bang. Someone screamed. Velvet covered her ears, suddenly afraid. Brick dust showered down from the shelter roof, covering everyone's hair and clothes.

Then, with a blink, the candles went out. And so did Mr Jackson's torch.

There was a beat between the bombs. Velvet felt the air change. The animals sensed it too. The barking, miaowing, scrabbling sounds grew frantic. Something fluttered past Velvet's head.

'Oh heck, my budgie's on the loose!' a woman called out. 'Can you catch her?'

'How are we supposed to do that, Doreen?' someone else snapped. 'We can't see further than our own noses!'

Even with the racket outside, you could hear a gasp, a squeal, as the bird landed on someone, then took off again. Velvet prayed the poor thing wouldn't make the mistake of landing near a cat, or a dog for that matter.

'I'm going to try and get it,' Lynn decided, scrambling to her feet.

Except suddenly everyone else had the same idea. The dark was full of moving things – a shoulder, an arm, outstretched hands. Velvet grew hotter and more afraid.

'Stop pushing!' she cried.

Worse were the dogs – all eight or so – who'd now whipped each other up into a deafening howl. In amongst the mayhem, the bombs kept falling: a high-pitched whistle, an almighty thump, more debris falling from the ceiling.

When things reached panic point, Mr Khan did the only thing he could do: he opened the shelter door. Cool night air flooded in as people tumbled up the steps and into the street. Velvet clung on to Lynn's hand. For a split second she was relieved to be out of the crush. Then, the smell of anti-aircraft fire and brick dust. The sky still thrumming with enemy planes. It felt like the end of the world.

Most people were now trying to get back into the shelter. Two lone figures and their dog – the Clementses – hurried off in the opposite direction down the street.

'That's right! Run away!' Mrs Gable shouted after them. 'Cowards, you lot are! Bloomin' cowards!'

Velvet didn't think they should've run away, either. But a *coward* was a harsh thing to call someone, especially in wartime.

'You're lucky I'm not sending you to court!' Mr Jackson yelled in Mr Khan's face. 'There are rules for the blackout. And you, *sir*, with your light showing and all the pets of Plymouth inside that shelter, have broken two of them!'

'I couldn't turn people away,' Mr Khan insisted. 'They didn't know the rules had changed.'

'I'm in charge here now, not that soft-touch Mr Perks.' Mr Jackson was blocking the shelter doorway.

'From now on, animals are banned. End of story.'

'Now hang on a minute!' Doreen the budgie owner cried.

Lynn looked at Velvet, alarmed. 'I can't leave Sprout on his own!'

Overhead, the German planes seemed lower and louder than ever. Anti-aircraft fire rattled across the city. It was dangerous to be out here, cowering in the gutter. Yet Velvet knew her friend wouldn't go back inside without her dog, and she'd be exactly the same if Sprout were hers. In fact, all the pet owners were now clutching their animals tightly and staring at Mr Jackson with real hate.

Maybe it was this, or the surge of panic, that made her rush up to Mr Jackson.

'You *have* to let us all back inside, Mr Jackson,' Velvet pleaded. 'Otherwise we might all die out here in the street and that'll be your fault.'

Mr Khan coughed.

Mr Jackson sized her up coldly. 'Is that so?'

His eyes went from her to the sky. The whistling sound came next, then a yell of 'Bomb incoming!' People and pets dashed for the shelter, and Mr Jackson, though he tried, couldn't stop them.

It wasn't the end of the matter, though, not by a long way.

3

The next day, with the smell of cordite still sharp in the air, a letter arrived on every Barton Street and Portland Place doormat. It was signed, in spiky ink, by a Mr Eugene Jackson. From now on the public shelter was for human use only. To save any future confusion, the new rule was there – in writing – for all to see.

'... owing to unprecedented demand for seating ...' Velvet read aloud to Lynn and Mo. Sprout was with them too, though not listening.

'But the Portland Place lot are only using our shelter because theirs got bombed,' Lynn pointed out. 'They won't be coming forever.'

'Let's hope the Germans won't, either,' Mo replied.

Velvet sighed. 'I just wish Mr Perks was still here. And Nipper.'

It was after school and they were walking towards the seafront. They often went down there when the weather was glorious, the salt smell of the sea making a pleasant change from brick dust and smoke.

Today the sea glittered gold in the sunshine. In the park overlooking it, Smeaton's Tower stood as majestic as ever, its red and white stripes as bold as a barber's pole. Years ago it'd been a lighthouse and on a very clear day you could still see its stumpy remains, miles out to sea on Eddystone Rocks. In Victorian times, when the rocks eroded, the lighthouse was brought back to Plymouth, and became a memorial to the man – Mr Smeaton – who'd invented it.

The nearest lighthouse now was at Budmouth Point along the coast, and that had been daubed with dull grey paint to camouflage it from German pilots. Velvet was glad the coastguards had left Smeaton's Tower alone – its bright colours were such an uplifting sight. If it survived Hitler's bombs then there was hope for the rest of them too. Today, though, Mr Jackson's letter was doing its very best to dampen her spirits.

'And ...' she read with emphasis, 'for reasons of hygiene and public health ...'

'Well, it does stink a bit down there with all those dogs,' Mo admitted.

Lynn glared at him. 'And *rats*.'

'Failure to comply will lead to a fine of £25 – crikey, that's gone up – or a court appearance,' Velvet read on. 'The possibility of custodial sentencing cannot be ruled out.'

Mo pulled a face. 'He means prison!'

Velvet, who still couldn't believe her own nerve at standing up to Mr Jackson last night, was worried. She'd need to be careful from now on.

Yet it was obvious they had to do something. The bombers would be back, if not tonight then very soon. There must be a way of keeping Barton Street's animals safe during an air raid.

They'd entered the park by now, with its beautiful views out over Plymouth Hoe. Lynn unclipped Sprout's lead so he could have a run about.

'Here's a good picnic spot,' said Mo, flopping down on to the grass. Between them, they'd clubbed together to buy one sticky bun, the icing of which was melting rapidly, and a bottle of lemonade.

Velvet sat beside him, and Lynn was about to when Sprout set off on little terrier legs across the park.

'Uh-oh, what's he seen?' she asked, staring after him.

'*Who's* he seen, more like,' Velvet replied, because Sprout was making a beeline for a boy and his scruffy grey dog.

Mo shielded his eyes from the sun. 'Isn't that . . .?'

'Robert Clements,' Velvet finished. 'With his pregnant dog.'

Picnic forgotten, Lynn and Velvet pelted across the grass. They reached Robert just as Sprout was going in for a nose nip.

'I'm ever so sorry,' Lynn panted, yanking him back by his collar. Velvet held him steady while she fastened his lead. He was still growling as she pulled him a safe distance away. 'Is your dog okay?'

There didn't seem to be any damage, but Robert's dog was snarling. She was a funny-looking creature – grey-haired and whiskery with giant knobbly paws. Her stomach looked rounder and fuller than ever.

'Lynn could check her over if you like,' Velvet offered. 'She knows heaps about animals.'

Robert pulled his dog protectively towards him. 'No, thanks very much. And by the way, your dog should be on a lead.'

He was right, of course – Sprout *was* a temperamental little toad. But for someone who'd caused a fair bit of trouble himself last night, Robert was sounding rather a prig.

'There's no need to get shirty,' Velvet replied hotly. 'We've said sorry. Anyway, you're a fine one to talk. It's because of you not pulling the curtain across properly at the shelter that we can't take pets down there any more.'

Robert stared at her, confused. '*What?*'

'Haven't you had the letter? Mr Jackson sent one to everyone.'

'Mum opens all our post,' he replied, the confused look now a worried one. 'What are we meant to do? Leave our pets on their own? Because I won't do it, not for anything.'

Velvet softened. Anyone who cared this much about his dog was all right in her book. She remembered how he'd stared at her mum that day in the street like she was some sort of saviour. Robert Clements wasn't *all* prig, she supposed.

'That's what we're trying to work out,' she explained. 'We need somewhere big enough for all Barton Street and Portland Place's pets – and their owners. Can you think of anywhere?'

'No, not everyone together. That won't work.' He'd started to back away. 'Count me out. I'll look after myself, thanks.'

Turning, he set off across the grass, the dog lolloping at his heels.

'How? What are you going to do?' Velvet called after

him. But he kept walking away from them as fast as
he could.

*

The incident left Velvet baffled. Robert Clements was
a bit of a strange one.

'Where's Mr Clements? Does anyone actually
know?' she asked as they rejoined Mo.

'Isn't he in prison?' Mo said. 'I'm pretty sure that's
what my mum said.'

Velvet didn't know. From what she'd seen it only
seemed to be Robert and his mum, and for some
reason people didn't much like them.

'Perhaps he's a murderer!' Mo gushed. 'He might've
chopped up people and made them into pies!'

Velvet laughed. 'That's Sweeney Todd, you goof.'

'He could be away fighting,' Lynn suggested. A lot
of people's dads had joined up to fight – Lynn's dad
had – so it seemed a very likely scenario.

Yet some dads went away for reasons other than
war, and sometimes didn't come back. Even the people
closest to them, who were supposed to know why,
couldn't always explain what had happened: this was
certainly the case whenever Velvet tried asking about

her own father. She was beginning to wish she'd not brought the subject up.

'Let's have our picnic, shall we?' she said.

The lemonade was lukewarm, the bun so sticky that with every mouthful they got equal parts paper bag and cake. Once they'd finished, it was back to the shelter business. Licking her fingers, Lynn pulled a notebook from her satchel. She carried it everywhere – pencil attached with string – and was forever making lists in it.

Velvet was still thinking about something Robert had said. 'It'll probably be best to start with just our street, won't it? If there's too many of us it might not work.'

Mo agreed. 'It'll be tricky to find a space big enough.'

So they decided, just for now, to stick with Barton Street.

'What do we need to know first?' Mo asked.

'Exactly how many animals we've got on our street,' Lynn replied.

One by one Velvet reeled them off. When the list was complete, Lynn showed them what she'd written in her notebook:

Pet name + type	House number	Owner's name
Bonzo, white cat (*deaf*)	4	Mrs Gladys Jones
Hattie and Helen, hens (*BEWARE! FIERCE!*)	6	Mrs Florence Gable
Joey, whippet (*shivers a lot, likes blankets*)		
Clarence, tortoise (*bites human toes*)	10	Mr Michael McKinley, Mrs Sheila McKinley
Kip, black cat with white paws (*hates Bonzo – see above*)		
Tansy, tabby cat (*moults badly*)	14	Miss Jane Billingham
Bill-Boy, Jack Russell (*chases cats*)	16	Mrs Ethel Snape
Muggins and Jeffrey, guinea pigs (*enjoy being brushed*)	22	Mrs Posy Archer
Dot, sausage dog (*tummy tickles please*)	28	Mr Ronald Huxley
Pickle, blue budgie (*likes sitting on people's heads*)	33	Mrs Doreen Miles
Pudding, ginger cat (*a cat bully, likes humans*)	17	Betty the pub landlady

Pet name + type	House number	Owner's name
Sprout, terrier cross (*likes carrots, hates big dogs*)	20	Miss Lynn Parsloe
Sherlock, black and white rat (*answers to his name*)	3	Master Mo Hussein

Next, they discussed potential places for the shelter. It was Lynn who brought up Mo's parents' cellar: theirs was the only house on Barton Street big enough to have one.

'Could you fit everyone in?' Lynn asked hopefully.

'Maybe,' Mo replied. 'Though I don't think my parents will be very keen on having dogs in the house.'

The old railway arches by the bus depot were another favourite, but these were open-fronted, like caves, and rather grim.

'It'd be super noisy,' Velvet worried.

'And stinky,' Lynn agreed.

Which brought them back to Mo's cellar.

'So you think your parents will say no?' Velvet asked. Mo's parents, very nice though they were, kept an immaculate home. Their hallway floor was so polished you could see your face in it. She doubted they would agree to their house being used as a shelter.

'And before you ask,' Mo said, reading her expression, 'I'm not doing it behind their backs.'

'But once your parents are at the public shelter, couldn't we sneak people in?' Velvet pressed him. 'They'd never know anyone had been there.' Though she knew it was a long shot. The state of the hallway floor would give the game away, if nothing else.

Lynn, who had her thinking face on, said nothing; it was Sprout who belly-crawled across the grass and nuzzled Mo's hand.

'All right!' he caved in. 'I'll give it a go: but don't blame me if I'm grounded till my eighteenth birthday.'

Velvet beamed. 'Next time there's a raid, then? Everyone to yours?'

'As a trial run,' Mo said very firmly. 'If it doesn't work out we find somewhere else, got it?'

'I'll spread the word on my way home,' Lynn decided.

With no lemonade left for a toast, they made do with a cheer. It was then Velvet noticed how everyone else in the park seemed to be staring and pointing at the sky.

'Wow! It's a dogfight!' Mo said, getting to his feet.

The aeroplanes were so high above them they were tiny glints of silver. Moving really fast, twisting, turning, trailing white smoke, it was as if they were writing messages in the sky.

'That's amazing!' Mo cried.

'Depends on who wins,' Velvet reminded him.

'Hitler's not finished with us yet,' mused Lynn. 'That's why all those American soldiers have been brought in.'

Velvet's mum had mentioned this the other day. A whole trainload of American GIs had set up camp at Budmouth Point, the place with the lighthouse just up the coast. They were expected here in Plymouth any day, and it made Velvet wonder why.

'Hitler's not going to invade us though, *is* he?' she asked.

''Course he won't,' said Mo. Seeing Velvet's pinched, worried face he pointed at the sky. 'See our chap up there? You think he's running out of fight?'

Velvet watched, hand over her mouth. It was horrible to think of the pilots fighting to the death. But she couldn't *not* look, either, and kept watching until the planes swooped away over the sea, out of sight.

4

A day later, the planes were back – bombers this time, so lumbering and heavy-sounding it seemed impossible to believe the sky could hold them up. By the time the siren went just after tea, all the pet owners on Barton Street knew exactly what to do.

The Plan – they still hadn't thought up a better name for it – was to wait ten minutes for the Husseins to leave their house. The back door was always unlocked, Mo assured them, so this was the way in – oh, and could everyone please take their shoes off. They'd find the cellar door on the right in the hallway, the cellar itself down some steps. And could they remember to tidy up any crumbs, sandwich wrappers, etc. afterwards, and absolutely NOT touch Mrs Hussein's jars of onion pickle, which were arranged on the shelves down there in strict date order. When the All Clear sounded they must leave *immediately*.

'Won't people notice if they're not at the public shelter?' Lynn had asked.

'They could use Mr Perks's excuse,' Mo replied.

'But he's staying at his sister's,' Velvet said, surprised. 'That's not an excuse, that's a fact.'

Mo shrugged. 'If you say so.'

'What d'you mean?' Velvet was suspicious.

'Only that he and Nipper were seen last night at the bus station.'

Which struck Velvet as rather odd.

*

The Plan started to go wrong almost straight away. After she'd waited the agreed ten minutes, Velvet went to Mo's. She wasn't expecting to find his parents still on the doorstep. Luckily, they hadn't seen her yet, so she hid in the neighbours' doorway and waited, holding her breath.

In amongst the footsteps, tutting, and – finally – the closing of the front door, the Husseins left the house. Her relief became panic when she realised Mo was with them. He wasn't meant to be. He was supposed to be here, with her, for when the pet owners arrived. So was Lynn.

She couldn't shout out and stop him, either. If the Husseins saw her lurking, the whole top-secret plan to use their cellar risked being blown. She sank deeper into the doorway, her brain reeling. And where was Lynn? She was never late for anything.

Had they agreed to meet here? Did anyone say as much? She really wasn't sure any more. There was no sign of the pet owners, either. A horrid sinking feeling came over Velvet that she'd got the wrong end of the stick.

Only the grown-ups with pets were coming. She didn't need to be here, nor did Mo, or Lynn. No one had actually said so because it was so obvious. Mo's parents would know if he wasn't at the shelter; so would Lynn's mum, who was off work with bronchitis. And as for the pet owners, well, of course she hadn't seen them: they'd been told to use Mo's back door, not the front.

Feeling stupid, frustrated and very near to tears, she set off for the public shelter. With any luck, Mr Khan would still let her in. Already, the first German planes were darkening the sky. She started to run.

Halfway up the street came a blinding flash. Instinct made her cover her head, but when she heard the familiar whistling sound, she knew it was too late.

A terrific *boom* made her ears pop. The ground shook. Velvet fell forwards on to her hands and knees.

This is it, she thought, *this is the bomb with my name on it.*

When the air cleared a little, she saw rubble blocking the entire road. A wall had come down – the front of someone's house by the look of it. There was glass everywhere, roof tiles, bricks and shreds of curtain, a singed rug.

But no more noise. No more planes. The sky was peaceful again but for the searchlights and the barrage balloons, floating in the dark like gigantic chefs' hats.

Velvet stumbled to her feet. Her hands stung and she'd cut her knee, but she wasn't badly hurt, just shaken and disorientated. The heap of rubble literally split Barton Street in half like a giant wall – the public shelter at one end, her at the other. There was no way of clambering over it. The whole lot looked smoky and hot as if it might, at any moment, burst into flames.

Then she saw the body.

It lay in the road just in front of her, close enough for her to see dust in the man's hair. The shock made her dizzy. There was a funny whooshing in her ears. She'd never seen a dead person before, and this one looked so lifelike she half expected him to move. He was wearing a khaki-coloured uniform and had, to her even greater surprise, skin darker than hers.

His hand was open, as if he was reaching for something he'd dropped: looking closer, she saw he had. Just beyond his fingertips was a little red jewellery box. Dazed, she picked it up, brushed the dust off. The lid opened with a tiny click. Inside, on satin padding, was a diamond ring.

'Hey! What you got there?' said a voice from the ground.

Velvet jumped out of her socks. 'Oh my word! You're alive!'

'I think so.' The man stood up shakily. It was like watching a ladder unfold – his long body seemed to go up and up. She had to blink to stop herself staring.

'May I have that, miss?' the man asked, pointing to the ring box. 'I must've dropped it when I fell.'

'Gosh, um, yes, sorry.' Flustered, Velvet gave it back to him. He looked very relieved, tucking it away in his shirt pocket and buttoning down the flap for good measure. She also noticed he had an accent – American, maybe?

'Now,' he said, bending a little so he was almost at her height. 'Can you point me in the direction of the docks?'

She nodded, aware she was still staring. 'You're a soldier, aren't you? An American one.'

He smiled. 'I'm Eddie Johnson, here with the United States Army, miss, and a little lost on my way back from ring shopping. And you are ...?'

'Velvet. The docks are just down—' She stopped, hearing engines. Not just the throb of one or two, but a whole skyful. 'Uh-oh, can you hear that?'

'Darned Luftwaffe!' Eddie cursed. 'We need to get us under cover, miss. Where's the nearest shelter?'

'That way.' She pointed at the blocked street. 'But I know a decent cellar that's much nearer.'

*

By the time they reached the backyard, bombs were coming down like hailstones. Thankfully, just as Mo promised, the door was unlocked.

'Come in, then,' Velvet said, when Eddie hesitated on the step.

'They'll think I'm missing. I'd better report back,' he answered, then stumbled forwards, a hand on his head. 'I'm sorry. I think I'm hurt.'

There was something wet running down the side of his face.

'You definitely need to come in,' she pleaded, tugging his arm. She'd no idea what she was going to do with him once she'd got him to the cellar, but it was the safest place to be by a mile.

Somehow, he stayed upright as Velvet led him inside. All the time the bombs kept falling, the windows rattling, the floor quaking under their feet. The house was very dark. She'd never been so relieved to find the hallway and the cellar door. Opening it, Velvet caught the familiar waft of Mrs Hussein's onion pickle. There was another smell too – sort of doggy.

As she helped Eddie down the steps, a small furry body hurled itself at her. It almost knocked her flying.

'Sprout!' Velvet knew the greeting immediately.

A sharp click in the dark as a torch went on.

'Looking after him for your pal Lynn, I am.' The speaker was Mr Huxley, owner of Dot the sausage dog, who was tucked snugly under his arm. 'Perhaps he'll settle now you're here.'

As her eyes grew accustomed to the torchlight, she could see seven, maybe eight people sitting against the far wall. They'd brought blankets, cake, tea and, of course, their pets. Dogs sat in their owners' laps, eyes glued to the food packets and the cat baskets that were being kept at a sensible distance on the opposite side of the cellar. Somewhere in the dark, a hen was clucking.

They were all here, Velvet saw with pride – and surprise. The Plan *had* worked.

'Who's this, then?' Mr Huxley's torch swooped across Eddie's face, then down to his feet. Mr Huxley whistled. 'Big fella, you are. Hurt your head too, by the looks of it.'

'Bring him over here,' called Betty. 'We'll sort him out.'

With Eddie lowered carefully to the floor, Barton Street's pet owners got to work.

Velvet hovered anxiously, torn between wanting to help and feeling a bit sick. She wasn't good with injuries or blood. In the end, she distracted herself with Mo's rat, Sherlock, whose cage was behind some coal sacks. She got him out, let him run up and down her arms, before putting him in her skirt pocket where he promptly went to sleep.

Meanwhile, with hot water from their flasks, Betty and friends cleaned up Eddie's head wound, then dressed it with a handkerchief, bound it with a stocking and gave him a cup of tea.

'With them Yankees at the docks, are you?' Betty asked him. 'Got caught out in the raid?'

'Yes, ma'am.' Eddie looked ashamed, as if being in the US Army he should know better.

'He was ring shopping,' Velvet explained.

Betty smiled. 'In that case, love, you're forgiven.'

For the next hour, poor Eddie was bombarded with questions: who was his intended? Had he asked her yet? What did she look like? When would they be married? Where would they live?

'My girl's called Queenie.' Saying her name made his whole face light up. 'My unit's leaving soon for Europe, and I want her to know I'm serious, that I'll be back for her, you know?'

'That's so lovely, that is,' Betty said.

When they'd passed the ring around and cooed over it, Mr Huxley cleared his throat as if he'd had enough soppy talk for one evening.

'How do you two know each other, Velvet? Some relative of yours, is he?' Mr Huxley asked. He meant their skin colour, which was what folks always saw first. Put two brown-skinned people together and they had to be related, though no one ever seemed to think it if you were white.

'No, he's not,' Velvet mumbled.

'Though I do have English family, sir,' Eddie told him.

'Oh well, then,' said Mr Huxley, looking confused.

Eddie gave Velvet's arm a very gentle punch, as if to say he was always hearing stupid assumptions about his skin colour, so he knew what it felt like. Though Velvet tried to smile, her eyes started to water. It was, she realised, the first time she'd met someone who truly understood.

Despite Mr Huxley being embarrassing, she let herself, just for a moment, imagine Eddie *was* one of her family – her dad or an older brother – and supposed it wouldn't be so bad. At least he'd promised his lady friend Queenie he'd come back. Later that night, when he had Sprout, Dot, Joey the whippet and Bill-Boy the Jack Russell all gathered round him begging for fuss, she saw he was a great dog lover too. And that, in a person, was always a good sign.

5

With a rat snoring in her skirt pocket, Velvet somehow fell asleep. She awoke to the sound of the All Clear. As people around her gathered their things, Mr Huxley's slightly stooped silhouette was already waiting in the daylight at the top of the cellar steps.

'Quickly now,' he said, hurrying them along.

On the way out, Velvet gave the hallway rug a straighten. Everything had to look exactly as the Husseins had left it.

'So long,' Eddie said, shaking her hand. He'd taken off the makeshift dressing. There was no blood on his face any more, but his right eye was puffing up nicely. 'Thanks again for saving me.'

She blushed. She hadn't saved him, she'd just known where they could shelter. If anyone had done the saving it was him, because she'd never slept right through an air raid before.

'You're getting a shiner,' she told him.

Once Eddie had gone, and she was wandering back to her house, Velvet suddenly remembered Sherlock. To her horror, he wasn't in her pocket any more. He must've crawled out in the night and the obvious place to look for him was the cellar. Knowing she didn't have long – minutes at the most – Velvet tore back into the Husseins' house. Now the blackout was over, and having found the cellar light switch, she flicked it on.

'Sherlock!' she called, moving between the pickle shelves, empty crates, an old bicycle, gardening implements. 'Come on, boy! Sherlock!'

For a rat who supposedly answered to his name, he wasn't being very obliging. Dispirited, she kept looking, but there were so many shadowy corners, so many gaps between the bricks where a rat could hide. She might be down here all day and still not find him. And that wasn't an option, either. She'd have to tell Mo.

She didn't see the blood until she almost slipped in it – a sticky, jam-like pool right by the back door. What made it ten times worse were the giant footprints that trailed across the kitchen floor towards the hall. Velvet groaned out loud. She and Eddie had forgotten to take their shoes off last night, hadn't they? Mrs Hussein was going to go bonkers when she saw.

Frantic, she searched the kitchen for a cloth. There was only a dry one, which didn't do much, and she didn't have time to draw water from the pump out in the yard. The pool of blood wouldn't shift at all. She ended up putting the doormat over the top of it. Feeling sick, and very sorry, she ran home.

*

By the time they reached school, Lynn knew everything, even the bad bit about Sherlock.

'I'm dreading telling Mo,' Velvet said.

'Best get it over with,' Lynn advised her. 'Here he comes now.'

He was heading straight for them across the school yard, his face as stormy as anything. Velvet gulped. His mother had seen the kitchen floor, hadn't she? Or maybe he'd found Sherlock's empty cage. Both things were her fault, and Velvet felt terrible.

'I'm really sorry, I tried to clean it up,' she blurted out, when Mo reached her.

'*You*, Velvet Jones, shouldn't even have been there!' he cried. 'What were you doing? And whose were those enormous footprints?'

She tried to explain about getting caught in the raid.

About Eddie and his bleeding head.

'My mum has to go to work today, and what is she doing instead? Scrubbing the kitchen floor!' Mo fumed.

'I'm sorry.' Velvet's eyes filled up.

'What did I tell you about shoes?' Mo went on. 'Take them off, I said, didn't I?'

Velvet nodded. 'I'd better go and help your mum.'

'Leave it.' Mo, taking a deep breath, grew calmer. 'My parents think someone broke in last night, that's all. I haven't told them the truth.'

'Phew!' Lynn gasped.

Velvet shut her eyes with relief.

'We can't do it again, though,' Mo warned. 'I said we'd try it, but it really hasn't worked. Next time the animals will have to go somewhere else.'

Lynn frowned. 'But *where*?'

'Your place was pretty perfect,' Velvet risked telling him. 'Everyone knew where it was, the animals were really settled – far more than they normally are at the shelter. We all got a good night's sleep.'

'Even Sherlock, eh?' Mo asked.

So he knew about that too: she felt absolutely rotten.

'He was in my pocket, honestly. I just wanted him to be all right, and feel safe, but when I checked in the morning . . .' Velvet trailed off. It was pointless trying to explain.

This plan of theirs wasn't working. They were just a bunch of kids who loved animals, and it wasn't enough. They weren't brave or skilled like Lynn's mum or Velvet's. They couldn't even think of a name for their plan, let alone agree on something that actually might work.

*

After school, Velvet knocked on every door in Barton Street *and* searched every single backyard. She was determined to find Sherlock. All day Mo had insisted that his pet rat would make his own way home, and that he wasn't really that worried. But he'd been stiff and quiet in class, and hadn't touched the semolina pudding at lunch, when normally he'd have gone back for seconds.

Lynn came searching with her. The blocked road made everything take longer. Once they'd done the top of the street – with no joy – they had to walk right round the neighbourhood to reach the bottom of Barton Street again, where at Velvet's house they found a parcel waiting on the doorstep.

'Someone's left you a present,' Lynn observed.

'Like who?' Velvet was wary: she couldn't think who'd send her a gift.

The box was a posh-looking shoebox – pale blue with gold lettering along the sides, the lid tied down with string. Since Velvet's last pair of shoes had been brought home wrapped in newspaper from the second-hand shop, it was a bit intriguing. Until she realised the box was just the right size for a dead rat. She started to feel ill then, because she was pretty certain Sherlock was inside.

Taking a deep breath, Velvet picked up the box. As she did so, she felt something moving about inside. It nudged against the lid, lifting it slightly. She glimpsed whiskers and a pink twitchy nose.

'Sherlock!' she gasped. 'Someone's found him! He's all right too!'

Except he wasn't. Once they'd got the lid off, they could see the damage properly. Poor Sherlock was holding up his front left paw in a very odd way. He was breathing too quickly. His eyes, usually as bright and black as jet beads, were misty and half closed.

'There must be something we can do for him?' she begged Lynn.

Lynn made a 'hmmmmm' sound, which meant she was thinking.

'You've got matches indoors?' she asked. 'Aspirin? String?'

'Errr, I think so.'

'Good. We'll need to use your kitchen?'

On tiptoe, they slipped inside. After her night shift, Mrs Jones was still asleep upstairs. Velvet hoped to heavens she wouldn't hear them. Waking her up in the daytime when she was working nights never had happy consequences.

'We'd best wash our hands,' Lynn said.

Using the pail of cold water on the draining board, they took it in turns to wash. When they'd shaken their hands dry, the floor was wet and the kitchen stank of Lifebuoy soap.

'Now what?' Velvet asked.

They stood at the kitchen table, on which the shoebox – rat inside – took pride of place.

'We're going to set Sherlock's leg,' Lynn said.

Velvet's eyebrows shot up. 'What, with *matchsticks* and *string*?'

'And the tiniest grain of aspirin for his pain,' she explained.

It sounded crazy. Lynn was level-headed and had read a lot of books, but she wasn't a vet, not a proper one.

'You think you can do it?' Velvet asked.

Lynn tightened her pigtail, pushed her glasses up her nose. She looked formidable, suddenly. 'Won't know until I try. Can you find those things for me, please?'

Velvet fetched matches and a ball of string from the kitchen drawer. The aspirin were in a little brown envelope on the mantelpiece. She crushed one with the back of a teaspoon, mixing the tiniest amount with a dab of jam.

'Give it to Sherlock, gently now,' Lynn instructed, beckoning her back to the table.

But she was nervous, her hands trembling. Mo would've made a better assistant than her; he wasn't squeamish like she was. She did her best at rubbing a jammy finger along Sherlock's little lips, though she'd no idea if he'd swallowed any.

'The matches, please,' Lynn said. 'We're going to set his leg.'

Velvet swallowed. '*We?*'

'I can't do it by myself,' Lynn replied, rather sharply. 'Now, hold his leg for me.'

Willing the wooziness in her head to clear, she did as Lynn asked. The matches were lined up, short lengths of string cut. Then Lynn said, 'Right, I'm going to straighten it. He might squeal.'

'I'll look away for this part,' Velvet muttered.

There was a squeak – only a little one – then Lynn said, 'There, that's done it.'

When she felt brave enough to look, it was all over. Lynn was winding the ball of string, a satisfied smile on her face. Inside the box, Sherlock lay fast asleep. His little left paw, splinted with matchsticks, stuck out awkwardly at his side. But he was alive, at least, thanks to Lynn and whoever had brought him back in a shoebox.

6

Mending Sherlock's leg made Velvet more determined. Animals didn't cause this stupid war, so it was unfair that they should suffer. When a warning went out on the radio the next morning that another air raid was expected, she insisted they walk to school via the old railway arches. That had been their original second choice after Mo's cellar, and the need to find another shelter was now urgent.

To reach the old arches, they had to go via Portland Place. Already it was hot again, but the sun was hidden by queer grey-green clouds, the air prickling with the promise of a thunderstorm. Velvet and Mo both wore their school sweaters tied round their waists. Lynn, who kept hers on to be neat, was red-faced and sweating.

The streets were busy with trucks, the sort that carried soldiers, which rattled alarmingly over the potholes as they went by. The troops were mostly

Americans: you could tell by their smart light-coloured uniforms, and how well fed they looked. Though Velvet kept an eager eye out for Eddie, she didn't see him. The local residents meanwhile were filling buckets with water or sand, and putting fresh tape up in windows to protect the glass. It was all a worrying reminder that another big raid was coming.

'Here, you'll never guess what,' Mo said, as if he'd just remembered something. They were walking up Portland Place, having passed Robert Clements's house.

'What?' Velvet asked.

Mo dropped his voice, glanced over his shoulder. 'I found out about Mr Clements.'

Velvet rolled her eyes: Mo could be a right old gossip sometimes. Though she had to admit she was pretty keen to hear this. 'Go on, then. Is he really a murderer?'

'Worse. Mr Clements is a conchie!'

Lynn's eyes went wide with surprise.

'He *is*?' Velvet pulled a face. A conchie was a Conscientious Objector, someone who refused to fight. There were other names too – nastier ones like 'yellow-belly' and 'coward', which might explain Mrs Gable's choice of insult that night at the shelter.

'He's got a university degree *and* a good job,' Mo told

them. 'But because he refused to fight on grounds of "conscience", the War Office has made him drive a bus.'

'A bus? What, here in Plymouth?' Velvet had expected Mr Clements to be more glamorous, somehow. This discovery was a bit disappointing.

'Yup. The one that goes all the way across the moors to Okehampton.'

'No wonder people don't like the Clementses very much,' Lynn mused.

'Robert's ashamed, I bet,' said Mo. 'I mean, wouldn't you be if that was your dad?'

'Maybe,' Lynn replied. 'Though at least he knows his father's somewhere safe.'

'At least he *knows* his father,' Velvet muttered, more to herself than anyone else.

Behind them came the sound of a motorbike rumbling up the road. As the rider honked his horn, they jumped out of the way to let the vehicle pass, but when it drew level it slowed right down.

'Hey, Velvet!' The rider was Eddie, with another soldier riding pillon behind him. 'How you doing?'

Velvet beamed, especially as Lynn and Mo now stared at her with something like awe.

'I'm all right, ta,' she said. 'Your eye's looking better.'

'Luckily!' He smiled. 'Last bit of shore leave coming

up and I'm seeing my girl Queenie. Can't propose looking like a clown, can I?'

The other GI with him then butted in, 'Say, do you kids know a boy who lives round here with a dog?'

'What sort of dog?' asked Lynn.

'Big hairy thing. The boy's got dark hair. His mom's reported him missing and we think we've just found him, but he's being stubborn as hell and won't come out.'

Velvet glanced at Lynn. At Mo. It sounded like Robert.

'Is he all right?' Velvet wanted to know.

'I reckon so,' Eddie said, glancing at his watch. 'But look, we've just been radioed to another job in Stonehouse, so we need some help here. Would you try to get him out for us?'

'All right!' Velvet agreed.

'Where is he?' Mo asked.

'Those old railroad arches just up the top of the street by the bus depot. And here, you'll need this.' Eddie handed Velvet his torch.

She didn't say they'd been going there anyway.

*

The railway arches were the sort of rundown spot where older kids often met at night to light camp fires or drink beer. They consisted of three tall brick arches that ran deep into the ground like open-fronted cellars and smelled worse than a privy. Just behind was the bus station, where the city's buses came and went at all hours, spluttering and spewing out fumes. It was a noisy, grotty sort of place.

Mo's cellar had definitely been a better choice to shelter in. Even so, Velvet couldn't help thinking you'd be safer here in an air raid than sitting it out at home.

'How do they know there's a boy in here?' Lynn went first, picking over the chip wrappers and empty bottles that lay ankle deep on the floor. Inside, the arch quickly narrowed down to head height, and had the look of a slimy-bricked Victorian sewer. A far wall, about thirty or forty feet in, marked its abrupt end. There was no sign of anyone or any dog.

'It might not even be Robert Clements,' Mo pointed out.

But Velvet was pretty sure it was.

Then, from deep inside the arch they heard a high-pitched squeal.

'What on earth's *that*?' Velvet cried. It sounded more like a rat than a dog.

'Puppies,' Lynn replied. She pushed her glasses up her nose. 'Newborn puppies, I reckon.'

Velvet swallowed nervously.

'Should we maybe leave them to it?' Mo asked, beginning to back away.

'NO!' Velvet and Lynn cried together.

It was decided Lynn should go first.

'You're almost a vet,' Velvet said. 'You might be able to help!'

Lynn gave her a worried scowl. 'Don't say that. You might jinx me.'

'You both mended Sherlock's leg so you're hardly useless, either of you,' Mo reminded them.

'Exactly.' Velvet handed Lynn Eddie's torch. It was a good one, like a thin, bright lighthouse beam sweeping over the walls.

The place stank of damp and rotting things. Walking was impossible: they had to clamber over the junk-littered floor. Mo, bringing up the rear, had already torn his school shorts. And since that first tiny squeal, they'd heard nothing more. It crossed Velvet's mind that Robert had heard them coming and was hiding.

At the far end, Lynn stopped. Torchlight danced across the back wall, picking up mould, smoke marks and what looked like a door – the sort made of several planks of wood nailed together.

'He's in there, isn't he?' Mo whispered.

To confirm it, there was another squeal. It went on longer this time, and they heard a voice saying, 'Good girl. Keep trying.'

Lynn opened the door.

At first, it was hard to see. Everything looked grey, shapeless, and there was a smell like metal and dog all mixed together.

'Robert?' Velvet said warily.

A rustling, scrabbling sound came from the corner.

'Go away, can't you?' The voice was a boy's. Robert's. She was relieved, then annoyed.

'Stop being so blinking snooty for a second,' she said. 'Your mum's reported you missing, and we've been sent here by the army to bring you home.'

The space they now stood in was little more than a cupboard. On the floor, on Robert's school blazer, his dog lay panting. One small, black, damp-looking puppy was nuzzling greedily at her belly. Robert crouched beside her, his face white in the torch beam.

'Go away,' he said again.

'You need to come home,' Velvet replied, more gently now.

Robert shook his head. 'Mum doesn't want us there. We had a big fight. She didn't want the puppies born inside the house. She said it was best for Wisp to be somewhere quiet by herself, but I couldn't leave her, I knew she was frightened.'

'Most people would use their back shed,' Mo muttered. 'Not come to a stinky old railway arch.'

'I would've done if we still had one – it's where Wisp normally sleeps. But ours got burned down last week,' Robert replied.

'It did,' Velvet said, remembering the raid. How lucky that Wisp didn't perish along with it. No wonder Robert had been so grateful to her mother in the street that day.

'We're not leaving here without you,' Mo said, still sounding bristly.

Though in his current state Robert clearly wasn't going anywhere. There was blood all up his arms, and what looked like dark green slime.

'Don't panic. That's all normal,' Lynn whispered to Robert, 'How long since the first pup was born?'

'Two hours, maybe three,' he said.

Lynn paused. 'Right. Well, that *isn't* normal.'

The dog started straining again. She whimpered, nosing Robert's hand like she wanted him to help, but

224

all he could do was smooth her head and talk gently to her. It was obvious how much he adored her.

'Can't we take her to a vet?' Mo asked, realising how desperate things were.

'Too late,' Robert replied. 'He's on the other side of town.' He and Wisp were both exhausted and looked ready to give up. Velvet wanted to shake him. If Wisp were hers, she'd carry her all the way across Plymouth if she had to.

But Lynn was already kneeling down next to Wisp, rolling up her sleeves. 'The next puppy's stuck, that's the problem,' she explained. 'We need to get it out.'

Robert stiffened. 'Please keep away from my dog!'

'If we don't do something, she'll die,' Lynn said bluntly.

Robert started to cry.

'Look,' Velvet spoke up. 'Lynn knows animal stuff. She reads books on it and everything. Yesterday she mended a rat's broken leg.'

'My rat, actually,' Mo added. 'And I'm very glad she did. Better a limping rat than a dead one.'

Robert almost brightened. 'You managed to save the little chap, then?'

Which struck Velvet as odd: what did *he* know about Sherlock? Then, in the torchlight she caught sight of his feet, and on them, a pair of very new-looking shoes.

'It was you!' she cried. 'You were the one who found Sherlock and put him in a shoebox!'

Robert admitted it was.

'Thank you!' Mo spluttered. 'I mean, really. It was very decent of you!'

Mo was looking at him now in a whole different way. And when Wisp reached out to Lynn and licked her hand, it seemed to win Robert over. Wiping his nose, he said, 'We'd best get on with it, then.'

'Sit up by her head and talk to her,' Lynn instructed Robert, then to Velvet, 'Untie your sweater. You're going to hold the puppy in it as soon as it comes out.'

Velvet did as Lynn asked. Though she was nervous, her brain felt sharp. *We can do this*, she thought. *We really can do this*. Glancing at Lynn's calm, clever face she felt sure of it.

'Right,' said Lynn, taking a deep breath. 'I'm going in.'

There was a twist, a squelch. Lynn heaved. Wisp pushed. Moments later what looked like a lump of kidney landed in Velvet's school jumper.

'Rub it,' Lynn told her. 'Clear the sac off its nose so it can breathe.'

Velvet rubbed. She watched in amazement as the slimy thing no bigger than a guinea pig squirmed and squeaked into life. She was still staring at it when Lynn nudged her.

'There's another one coming, get ready!'

Before long, they'd delivered another black puppy, bringing the total to three. Then, just as Wisp was getting up to stretch herself and sniff Robert's pockets for food, she started shaking again.

'Watch out!' Velvet cried. 'There's one more!'

The puppy came out very fast. It was smaller than the others, with white on its face and paws. To Velvet, it was the most adorable of the lot. Yet although she rubbed it vigorously, the pup didn't move.

'We've saved Wisp and got three healthy ones, so that's something,' Lynn, tried to reason.

Mo, who'd kept quiet in the background all the way through, shuffled alongside Velvet. 'C'mon, let's give it one last shot.'

While Mo rubbed, she breathed into its bright pink muzzle. It didn't work. When Wisp turned around, realising there was another puppy, she gave it a sniff, a tentative lick. And then, very gently but firmly, she cleaned the pup from nose to tail tip. Like Velvet and Mo, she didn't give up.

Finally, the puppy's paws twitched. It coughed. A tiny tongue appeared. Velvet, tears rolling down her cheeks, watched as the puppy wriggled towards its mother's belly and started to feed.

Mo flung an arm round Robert's shoulders, grinning. 'We did it!'

'Thanks, all of you,' Robert said, and for the first time Velvet had ever seen him do so, he smiled.

7

Outside in the thundery daylight, Lynn remarked that they'd better go home to wash, since their bare arms and school shirts were looking rather stained.

'We ought to speak to Robert's mum too,' Mo said. 'Tell her he's safe.'

It was mid-morning, the road hot and noisy with shoppers and soldiers. Buses swinging in and out of the station made Velvet wonder if any of the drivers was Mr Clements, like Mo had told them.

Her excitement at the newborn puppies was wearing off too. She felt sweaty and tired, and could suddenly see only problems: four new puppies to keep safe, when they hadn't yet found a shelter for the existing pets. The railway arch was out of the question for tonight: they couldn't bring other people and animals here when the pups were so young.

They didn't even have a proper name for this idea of theirs, either, still calling it The Plan. Which was a joke, when they didn't have one.

Deep in thought, Velvet didn't see the bus pull into the kerb or Mr Perks step off it. She did, however, recognise Nipper. And Nipper, seeing her, swaggered across the pavement to her, dragging Mr Perks in his wake.

'Oh, Mr Perks! Oh, Nipper,' Velvet cried, crouching down to fuss the dog's ears and receive a faceful of licks. 'I'm so glad to see you both!'

It hadn't occurred to her that they might come back to the city. And yet here they were, like an answer to her prayers. With Mr Perks as warden again, there'd be no need for Mr Jackson. All the pets could come back to the public shelter. Everyone would be safe together.

The others were clearly thinking the same.

'Welcome home, sir,' Lynn said, struggling not to squeal in delight.

'A decent air-raid warden at last,' Mo chipped in. 'Good to see you, Mr Perks.'

'Well, well,' said Mr Perks, a little surprised. 'This is quite a welcome, young people!'

Velvet rushed on hopefully. 'So you'll be on duty tonight, won't you – if there's a raid?'

'No, not me.' Mr Perks rocked back on his heels. 'That warden business wasn't doing me any favours.

For the good of my health, I've had to retire.'

'What?' Velvet was horrified. 'But you can't! I mean – we need you!'

'Oh crikey,' muttered Mo. 'Now what do we do?'

Lynn frowned. 'But you are *back* from your sister's, aren't you, Mr Perks?'

'For now, yes,' he said. 'But I'll be going there tonight if there's a raid. Best place to be, if you ask me.'

It sounded as if Mr Perks had been coming to and from the city a fair bit recently, which was probably why Mo had seen him at the bus station the other day. Getting to her feet, Velvet noticed he looked healthier for it too, as if he'd had a few decent meals and spent time in the sunshine.

'You've not been *staying* with your sister, then?' Velvet asked.

'Good heavens, no!' He chuckled. 'I like my own bed too much. What I do is go there when there's an air-raid warning. There's a decent bus service out that way, and quite nice up on the moors it is, these summer nights. You're safer up there than down here.'

Velvet was thrown. So was Lynn, who was staring at Nipper with narrowed eyes.

'Do you take your dog on the bus?' she asked. 'The driver doesn't mind?'

Mr Perks rubbed his chin. 'Funny you should say that, love, because the last bloke did. But this new driver is a gem. He's a bit posh, like – he's a conchie who's been made to do the job. But he's proper decent about animals and says he'll take anyone's pets if it helps.'

Lynn looked at Velvet. 'Do you think . . .?'

But Velvet had already thought it. The man was Mr Clements. Had to be.

'How big is his bus?' she asked hurriedly. 'Could it take, say, fifteen people and their pets?'

'Well . . . I suppose so . . .' Mr Perks frowned a little. 'Why? That Jackson chap not letting animals in the public shelter?'

'No, he isn't,' said Mo.

'He's hateful,' Lynn stated.

'And looks like a ferret,' Velvet added.

Mr Perks tried not to laugh. 'Listen, if you tell people to get here for the five o'clock bus, we'll see what we can do.'

They all nodded eagerly. It had to be worth a shot.

*

By quarter to five that evening, the pavement outside the bus station was full. There were the usual office workers, secretaries, shoppers. And in amongst them dogs, a box of cross-sounding hens, some cats, guinea pigs, a budgie carried in a handbag, and of course all their owners. Velvet, Lynn, Sherlock and Sprout were there too. For the sake of appearances, Mo had stayed behind with his parents.

'Best of luck,' he'd said, trying to hide his disappointment. 'Here, Sherlock's safer with you.' And he'd handed over his rat in his little splint, which made Velvet feel guilty again, but also very glad that Mo had forgiven her enough to trust her.

When the bus pulled up and the driver opened the doors, Velvet saw straight away her guess was right. The man with dark hair and nervous hands was an absolute spitting image of Robert. If any of the Barton Street residents recognised Mr Clements, they didn't say. They all got on the bus, shared a few pleasantries about their pets, then took their seats. Mr Perks was at the front, Nipper at his feet.

'If the seat's free, Mr Perks, I don't mind if the old boy sits up with you,' Mr Clements said, which made Velvet rather like him.

On Mr Clements's left cheek was a very gruesome scar. He might've done a fair bit of fighting in the previous war, she supposed. And like Mr Perks, for the good of his health, he couldn't face doing it again. Though she still wondered why he wouldn't fight Hitler, she realised too that things were often more complicated than they first seemed.

Just as the bus was about to drive away, a motorbike pulled alongside it. Jumping from the bike, a soldier in US Army uniform ran to the bus and banged urgently on the door. A moment later Eddie was on board, scanning the rows of passengers.

'This is the animal evacuation bus, right?'

'I believe you could call it that,' Mr Clements replied.

'Good.' Eddie nodded, then spotted Velvet and Lynn. 'Hey! Listen, you kids. I've got to thank you for helping today. You did what we couldn't do, and you were truly awesome.'

Velvet knew she was going crimson. All the passengers were staring at her and Lynn, twisting in their seats or straining forwards, nudging each other.

'What did they do?' Mr Clements asked. 'Something brave?'

Eddie smiled proudly. 'Let's just say they found a missing boy and brought four amazing puppies into the world.'

Velvet glanced nervously at Mr Clements. Did he guess who Eddie was talking about? Certainly, there was a redness spreading up his neck. And he might've had rather watery eyes, but it was hard to tell from where she was sitting.

Thankfuly Eddie's attention had quickly moved on to Sprout and all the other animals cuddled in to laps and standing in the aisle. 'Man, back home we go everywhere on buses with our dogs, our chickens, even our hogs for market. Greyhound buses we call 'em. They go from town to town, state to state—'

'Fascinating, I'm sure,' interrupted a man in an office suit a few seats back. 'But can we get going now, driver, or we'll never make it home.'

With a final thank you, Eddie departed. As the bus wound its way out of the city streets, the idea came to Velvet.

'That's it!' she said to Lynn. 'We should call it Operation Greyhound.'

Lynn raised an eyebrow. 'What, The Plan?'

Velvet nodded. 'Because this is the plan now, isn't it? We can't find anywhere to shelter in Plymouth so we're getting out of town – on a bus.'

'And if it's a secret plan, then it needs a code name,' Lynn said, warming to the idea. 'One that Mr Jackson won't guess.'

It was the perfect name.

*

That night there was a thunderstorm. Rain fell in curtains across the moor, hissing over the scorched bracken before sweeping down towards the sea. At times, when the lightning was behind the clouds, it didn't look that different from a bomb blast. The thunder that came with it was almost as loud.

Down in the city the raid wasn't as heavy as expected, though there was enough action to make the view from the moor spectacular. It was like looking down on a board game or a tablecloth, all spread out before them. In amongst the dark shapes and flashes, loud bangs and orange glows, Velvet thought of her mum working hard. She did miss having a mother who was around at home, who might cook supper sometimes or tuck her into bed at night. But mostly she was proud of her overall-wearing, bucket-carrying mum who was doing her bit to keep the city – and its pet dogs – safe.

Mr Clements and his bus stayed with them through the storm, so they at least had somewhere dry to sit. They shared cake, flasks of tea, games of cards and silly stories. And to Velvet's delight Nipper insisted on plonking himself on her lap.

Though, it was funny how being out of the city made her feel almost homesick. All evening she thought of the others still down there – Mrs Parsloe driving her ambulance, Mo in the shelter, Robert, Wisp and those tiny puppies, most of all that little one with the white paws and chest. She really shouldn't have been thinking about him, but she couldn't help herself, though no good would come of it.

8

Yet, she had to ask, though it took Velvet a while to work up the courage. In her heart, she already knew what her mother's answer would be, but it didn't stop her trying. Nor did it help that these past weeks she kept visiting Wisp and her puppies at their home in Portland Place, and named the little white-pawed one Bertie after her long-dead grandad.

'No, no, and for the last time, no,' said Mrs Jones when her daughter finally brought the subject up, at a rare moment when they were sitting down for supper together.

'Why not?' Velvet pleaded.

'It'll bark all day when I'm trying to sleep,' Mrs Jones replied. 'And you know I don't really like dogs.'

'But I do,' Velvet tried to tell her.

Mrs Jones put down her fork. 'Dogs need feeding and walking every single day. And what about its toilet business? What if it gets sick?'

'I'll look after it.'

'Will you?' Mrs Jones asked. 'You can't even be trusted to get yourself to the air-raid shelter.'

Velvet sighed. She'd been expecting her mother to say something about that.

'Yes, Mr Jackson told me.' Mrs Jones glared. 'You've been missing rather a lot, apparently. He keeps a register of everyone's absences and you're not the only one who's been missing, either.'

Velvet opened her mouth, then shut it quickly. Telling her mum about Operation Greyhound would only get her into more trouble. But it wasn't fair. Why was it only supposed to be grown-ups who helped the war effort? At least Eddie had trusted them to find Robert and Wisp that day – and they done a decent job of it too.

She stabbed her meat pie, trying hard not to cry. Yesterday, Mrs Clements had put an advert in the window of the corner shop, saying 'Pups for sale – two boys, two girls – to loving homes only'. Though there was an unspoken understanding that Bertie was Velvet's, if she couldn't actually have him, then someone else would have to.

*

Lynn was having better luck with her mum. Somehow word had got to her about Sherlock's mended leg and Wisp's difficult delivery, and though Mrs Parsloe had always hoped her daughter would do a clean, safe job like being a teacher or an office manager, she was enormously proud.

'This vet business you're so set on?' she'd said. 'We need to have a proper chat about it. See what training you'll need.'

'The funny thing is,' Lynn confessed to Velvet when they were alone, 'I'd not the foggiest idea what I was doing when I delivered the pups!'

'But you thought it through and *did* it,' Velvet reminded her. 'And it worked.'

She just wished she could use the same approach on her own mother.

Even Robert had won his mother round. Back home in Portland Place, Wisp and her pups were given pride of place in the Clementses' kitchen. When Velvet visited she'd sit cross legged on the floor, cuddling, cleaning, feeding puppies, especially Bertie, who had a knack for climbing up her chest and falling asleep right underneath her chin. He smelled so sweet it made her mouth water.

But now the time was fast approaching when she

was going to have to say goodbye to him, and she wasn't
sure she'd be able to.

*

A few days later, Robert called by with the news she'd
been dreading.

'Try not to get upset, but someone's coming to look
at the puppies tonight,' he told her.

Velvet gulped. 'Who?'

'A man. He's after two pups, apparently.'

Once they'd got to know Mrs Clements, they
discovered she was very nice – not a bit like their own
sharp-eyed mothers who never missed a trick. But one
thing Mrs Clements was strict about was finding good
homes for the puppies.

'Do you want to come along and meet him?' Robert
asked.

Velvet thought it over. Either way it was going to be
agony.

'I'll be there,' she decided. It was better than pacing
the floor at home.

*

The man, when he arrived – late and smiling his apology – was none other than Eddie the American soldier. Mrs Clements showed him out to the kitchen, where Velvet, Lynn and Robert were chatting anxiously.

Straight away, Robert recognised Eddie as the soldier who'd tried – and failed – to persuade him to leave the railway arches and go home and stammered a 'hullo'. Lynn shook his hand again. Velvet tried to smile: she knew how much Eddie loved dogs, but it still pained her to think he might choose Bertie.

'To be very clear,' Mrs Clements told him, 'these dogs are pets, not military animals. They absolutely must have loving homes.'

Eddie nodded. 'I understand that, ma'am. The puppies aren't for me. They're for two young pals of mine who I know – just *know* – will treat your dogs right.'

While Robert sat with Wisp, Eddie was shown each of the puppies. They'd grown to the size of cats by now, and were going to be rough-haired like their mum. As they bounded about the kitchen on their too-big paws, it was impossible not to love them. But when Eddie picked up Bertie, Velvet's heart pinched.

'Not him!' she wanted desperately to say. 'He's taken!' But instead, she had to stand there, swallowing the words.

In the end Eddie couldn't choose, and said he'd be back tomorrow. Initially, Velvet was relieved. But she knew it was only prolonging the agony.

*

At home, she found her mother crying in the kitchen. She was so taken aback she didn't know what to do. Mrs Jones never cried, and didn't encourage it in others, either. Yet here she was, blowing her nose and weeping loudly.

'Mum?' Velvet said tentatively. 'What's going on?'

The best tea service was on the table, indicating someone had visted while she'd been out. Patting the place beside her, Mrs Jones made Velvet sit down.

'Mr Clements and that nice Mr Perks ...' her mother said, her voice wobbling. 'Came around ... telling me ... about the bus ... and the animals ...'

'Oh.' Velvet's face grew hot. '*That.*'

She took a deep breath. Her mother already knew bits and pieces, but the whole story was bound to come out sooner or later. It was a miracle they'd kept it secret for so long. Readying herself for the telling-off of a lifetime, Velvet was shocked when instead her mum reached for her hand.

'You brave, brave girl,' Mrs Jones sniffed. 'To think

243

you did something like that for all those people.'

'And their pets,' Velvet added.

Mrs Jones sat back in her seat, wiping her eyes and looking long and very hard at her daughter. 'You've grown up this summer, haven't you? Right under my nose and I hadn't even noticed.'

'You've been busy,' Velvet said. 'There's a war on, remember?'

Her mum smiled. 'That doesn't mean you're not important to me, Vee. You've had to look after yourself, be here by yourself for nights on end. No wonder you wanted something to do. You must've been pretty lonely.'

'I suppose I was,' Velvet admitted. 'But I've got brilliant friends – and they've got the sweetest pets. And if I can't have my own, then—'

'Oh, stop with your pleading, child!' Mrs Jones, laughing, held up her hands. 'I give in.'

Velvet gaped at her. 'You *what*?'

'You could do with the company, I see that now,' her mum acknowledged. 'And you must promise to look after it – mind you, you're doing a pretty decent job of it with everyone else's pets already.'

Velvet seized her chance. 'Is that a yes, then? *Is* it?'

Reluctantly, against her better judgement, Mrs Jones said it was. Before she had tea, before she changed out of her school things, and definitely before Eddie returned with his decision, Velvet raced round to Robert's house with her news. Bertie, finally, officially, was hers.

*

By the end of summer, the puppies were old enough to go to their new owners, including the young friends of Eddie's. One girl pup went to a boy in Somerset, the remaining male pup just up the coast to Budmouth Point. The final home proved a big surprise – bigger even than Mrs Jones's change of heart.

'Old Ferret-face wants a *dog*?' was Velvet's reaction.

It seemed he did. It'd made him rethink the air-raid shelter business too, though Velvet suspected that was Mrs Clements's work, bargaining the very best deal for her puppies.

Meanwhile, going to the park after school became an everyday part of life. It was what responsible dog owners did, and Bertie, now the size of a small calf, needed all the exercise he could get. It was amazing how much energy he burned chasing Sprout and Wisp, and, when he got bored of that, Mo's football.

On this particular day, Robert had received two messages in the post, which he was keen to share.

The first was a proper letter, postmarked 'Frostcombe', and read:

Dear Mrs Clements and Master Robert,

The pup arrived safely on Eddie's motorcycle last Wednesday, which happened to be my birthday. What a surprise! I've never had such a brilliant present!

I've named her Muffin because that's what she likes eating. It's better than what my bossy sister wanted to call her. (Lilac?! Really???)

Earlier this year our house got bombed, so at the moment we're living in a place called Frost Hollow Hall. It's seriously MASSIVE, with parkland and woods, and lots of other dogs. And there's a nice old lady called Tilly who feeds Muffin cake, so you really don't need to worry about her. Muffin is happy and I am too. So is my little sister Maggie. She says Muffin is going to be the size of a horse, though I think that's only next to the sausage dogs that already live here.

Yours very sincerely,
Stanley

The second was a postcard with a picture of the Budmouth Point lighthouse on the front, back in the days when it was bright red and white.

HELLO

Just so you know, Otter is a genius. He can shake paws, roll over, and fetch socks. I'm now teaching him how to climb the lighthouse ladder. Queenie, who's going to marry Eddie the American, says I'm to invite you all for tea. I hope you like mock banana sandwiches.

CHEERIO
Cliff

They had no idea what mock banana sandwiches were, but it was wonderful to hear about the pups.

'Muffin and Otter,' Velvet mumbled the names out loud. 'Hmmm.'

'Makes you think of small, sweet dogs, doesn't it?' Lynn mused as they sat on the bench, watching Bertie tear around the park. In reality, he was starting to look more like a wolf.

'He's got to be some sort of hound, hasn't he?' Velvet asked.

Robert laughed. 'He is – at least, Wisp is. Part deerhound, part whippet, part greyhound.'

'And there was me, thinking they were just scruffy old mongrels,' Mo said.

Velvet nudged him. 'To you they might be!'

To her, the word greyhound meant more than Wisp and her pups, more even than Bertie. It meant Eddie, and the air raids, and thunderstorms on the moors. Best of all it meant finding your way home again when the bombs fell silent at last.